# The BIRD SINGERS

'A totally thrilling, mysterious adventure'
**Michelle Harrison**,
Bestselling author of *A Pinch of Magic*

'Dark, intoxicating, so full of killer twists I didn't know who
to trust! This is an exciting, highly original debut from
a great storyteller'
**Emma Carroll**,
Bestselling author of *Letters from the Lighthouse*

'*The Bird Singers* is a gloriously dark fantasy from an exciting
new voice. A magical adventure with friendship and family at its
heart. Eve Wersocki Morris's debut is one to look out for!'
**Liz Kessler**,
Bestselling author of *When the World Was Ours*

'A captivating story, full of intrigue'
**Abi Elphinstone**,
Bestselling author of *Sky Song*

'Polish folklore meets the Lake District in a page-turning
mystery. I devoured it in one gulp'
**Phil Hickes**,
Author of *The Haunting of Aveline Jones*

'A deliciously spine-tingling story with sisterhood at its heart.
I loved it'
**A.F. Steadman**,
Au

# the BIRD SINGERS

## EVE WERSOCKI MORRIS

Hodder
Children's
Books

HODDER CHILDREN'S BOOKS

First published in Great Britain in 2022 by Hodder & Stoughton

1 3 5 7 9 10 8 6 4 2

Text copyright © Eve Wersocki Morris, 2022

ISBN 978 1 444 96332 8

Typeset in Egyptian 505 BT by Palimpsest Book Production Limited,
Falkirk, Stirlingshire

Printed and bound in Great Britain by Clays Ltd, Elcograf S.p.A.

The paper and board used in this book are made from
wood from responsible sources.

MIX
Paper from
responsible sources
FSC
www.fsc.org   FSC® C104740

Hodder Children's Books
An imprint of Hachette Children's Group
Part of Hodder & Stoughton Limited
Carmelite House
50 Victoria Embankment
London EC4Y 0DZ

An Hachette UK Company
www.hachette.co.uk

www.hachettechildrens.co.uk

For Alice

My sister. My best friend. My constant ally.

*Lean in! To hear a tale of dark misdeeds.*

*A cunning foe – a villainess – draws near . . .*

*Released from myth, she prowls with feathered tread.*

*Mistrust her human face – monster she does be.*

LOWESDALE
E
N
S
W
LOWESDALE GIANT
T.S.'S EMPORIUM
BOAT CAFÉ
LOWESDALE BOATING CENTRE
AVERY ISLAND

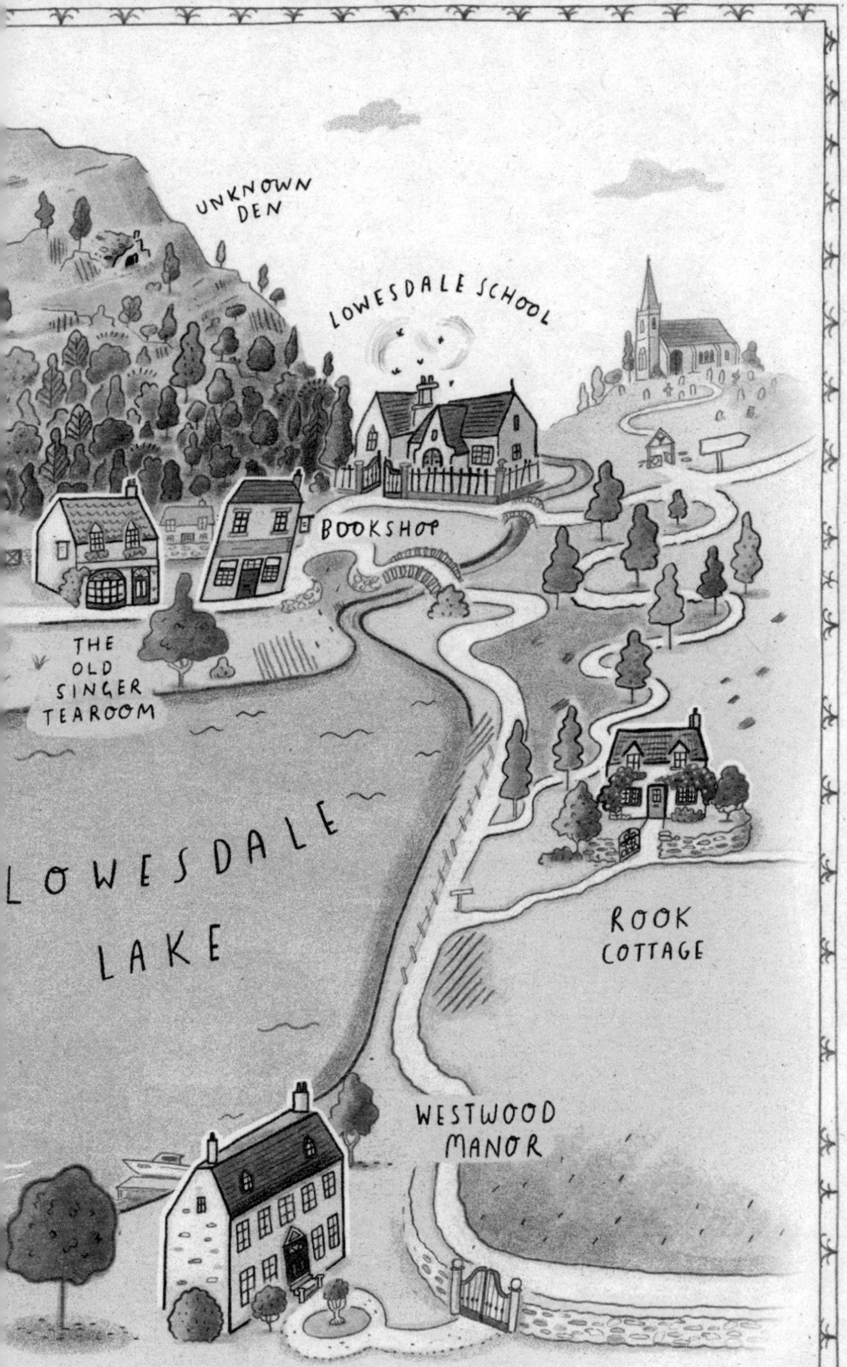
UNKNOWN DEN
LOWESDALE SCHOOL
BOOKSHOP
THE OLD SINGER TEAROOM
LOWESDALE LAKE
ROOK COTTAGE
WESTWOOD MANOR

# CHAPTER ONE

It wasn't the first night Layah had heard the whistling – but it was the first time she had followed it. She had been sleeping badly ever since they had arrived at the cottage by the lake. Perhaps it was the echoing silence of the countryside, nothing like the familiar hum of London at night. Perhaps it was sharing a room with her younger sister, Izzie, who snuffled in her sleep. Or maybe she was still sore at her mum for changing their holiday plans and dragging them to this soggy corner of nowhere.

It always started at midnight. At first, Layah thought it was birdsong – a high, thin sound that became a melody, rising and falling. And each night, it returned. Layah hadn't mentioned the whistling to her mum or Izzie. It made her shiver under the duvet but she would roll her pillow over her ears and eventually drift off to sleep.

Tonight, though – their third night in the cottage –

the whistling was different.

Layah's eyes were open but she couldn't remember waking or falling asleep. She lay in bed, her muscles tensed, listening. When the whistling came, it was more confident than before, wild and tuneful all at once. Her skin prickled, the way it used to during Babcia's bedtime stories about ghouls and witches. But Layah had stopped believing in monsters long ago. She refused to let her imagination run away with itself; fanciful daydreaming was Izzie's talent. Layah was going to find out where the whistling was coming from and silence her irrational fears.

She padded across the floorboards and unhooked the latch on the bedroom door. Out in the corridor, she peered into the pool of darkness below. The whistling was louder now, seeping through the house from somewhere outside. Layah creaked down the stairs, squinting against the patchy gloom. It sounded like it was coming from the back garden. As Layah pushed open the kitchen door, it squeaked.

The whistling stopped.

Her heart was thumping as she gazed across the murky kitchen towards the window. The garden was a mess of overgrown rose bushes and the sky was grey, offering little light, but she was certain there was a shape in the middle of the lawn. She moved closer to the window. There was something out there and it was human in outline, Layah was sure of it. Her fingers reached for the switch to the outdoor lamp – light sprang into the garden and there, staring straight back at Layah, was an old woman with blank, yellow eyes and a hungry, twisted smile. Layah screamed.

'Layah!' The kitchen light burst on and her mum came skidding into the room. 'Layah, what's wrong?'

Layah stumbled back to the window. The outdoor lamp flooded the back lawn. There was no one there.

'Mum, I – I thought I saw someone – just there.' Layah was breathing too fast to speak.

Her mum scanned the garden.

'I'm sure it was nothing,' she whispered.

'I thought – I thought I heard whistling—'

'Whistling?' Her mum seized Layah's shoulders. 'What did she look like? Layah, tell me what you saw.'

'It was a woman – she had these huge yellow eyes and long white hair,' stammered Layah, alarmed by the panic in her mum's face. Her mum released her and checked the lock on the back door.

'Mum, what's wrong?' Layah demanded. 'Was she real?'

Layah's mum turned and smiled, her bright eyes sombre.

'There's no one there, Layah. It was just a dream. Nothing to worry about.'

Layah wanted to argue but her head felt woolly with tiredness. Her mum placed an arm around her shoulders and shushed her upstairs and back into bed.

The whistling did not return. As Layah curled up under the covers, she heard only the hushing of the rose bushes and the lone cawing of a bird.

# CHAPTER TWO

Layah woke to a clattering of spoons and cereal bowls from downstairs. For a moment it felt like she was back in Babcia's house – on the camp bed in the study, surrounded by towers of books. Layah opened her eyes and saw the faded beige wallpaper of their holiday cottage and the grey light of Lowesdale. Her heart sank.

This time last year, they'd all been in Poland – her, Izzie, their mum and dad – on a proper family holiday visiting their grandmother. Babcia made every meal a celebration. For breakfast, they would make *pierogi* on the kitchen table; Babcia was always in charge, Layah and Izzie filling the doughy parcels with sauerkraut and mushrooms, their mum boiling them and their dad frying them in butter. They ate in their aprons, flour on their cheeks, all laughing at one of Babcia's stories.

This was their first summer without her and already everything was changing.

Layah's home in London was suddenly full of closed

doors, snappy conversations and hurried meals. No one seemed to have any time any more. Layah's family no longer had film nights, weekend outings or Sunday lunches. And Layah found herself spending more time alone in her bedroom – her parents were wrapped up in their squabbles and Izzie had her books.

Layah rolled over and checked her phone. No messages. Clearly her school friends were too busy having fun to notice she'd gone. She threw down her phone and opened the box on the bedside table. It was Babcia's final gift: an amber pendant on a gold chain. One for each of her granddaughters. Layah fastened the necklace around her neck, grabbed a jumper and headed downstairs.

Rook Cottage was – to put it mildly – cosy. As you entered one room you were already halfway into the next, and every inch was stuffed with flowery furniture. Izzie was reading at the kitchen table, a spoon of cornflakes dangling in one hand. Her dirty-blonde hair was pulled into two unbrushed plaits and she was blissfully unaware that the ends were dangling in her orange juice. Outside, Layah could see their mum untangling the washing line, the garden flowers nodding in the wind. A shiver ran through Layah, as she remembered her dream – that woman with yellow eyes smirking at her through the window. Layah gave her head a little shake.

She sat down next to Izzie and filled a bowl with chopped banana, cornflakes, chocolate flakes and Nutella – a family speciality – and tried not to think about her nightmare.

'You need the honey?' said Izzie, handing it over without glancing up from the page.

'Thanks.' Layah grinned. 'So what's new?'

'Reading.'

'Not much then,' muttered Layah, prodding her cereal as gloom engulfed her again.

This Lake District holiday might have been less boring if Layah's younger sister wasn't a walking bookstand. Today's book choice had a magical creature splashed across the cover.

There was a startled cry from the garden and Layah jumped as a mass of blackbirds took flight and the washing line whipped out of their mum's hands. Their mum threw a mouthful of bad words at the birds then stomped indoors. Ren Bellford wore a silk scarf to tie up her wild, dark hair and as usual she looked effortlessly radiant. Layah and Izzie both agreed it was detrimental to their education having a mum most of their teachers fancied. Their mum had insisted on giving her daughters her own surname, 'the responsibility of

7

an only child', she'd always claimed. Izzie looked like their dad – small and pale – but Layah had her mum's dark hair and eyes.

'I can't get the washing line pole to stand up!' announced Mum, shutting the back door behind her. 'We'll have to dry our clothes in the oven!'

'Bad idea,' advised Layah quickly. Their mum could burn pasta, so who knew what she'd do to their socks!

Their mum went to the fridge and took a glug of orange juice from the carton. 'I've fixed the hot water,' she continued, 'but now the toilet's making funny noises – maybe I shouldn't have kicked it . . .'

'We can help, you know,' said Layah, 'we're not babies.'

'Oh, I know.' Mum smiled. 'But I've got it. You two should be having a nice time. It's the summer holidays after all!'

'It's not really a holiday, though . . . without Dad,' said Izzie quietly.

Their mum's face crumpled as she looked at her daughters. Layah noticed dark circles under her eyes.

'You know how important your dad's work is to him,' Mum sighed. 'If a crusty old scientist in Denmark is giving a speech about ferrets with fevers or whatever-it-is, your dad says he has to be there!'

'I thought we were all going out for dinner on my birthday,' said Layah, 'to that fancy Polish restaurant with the red tablecloths. That was the plan.'

'Plans change,' said Mum lightly. 'We can still celebrate your birthday here – it's not until next week.'

'We're going to be here for my birthday?' Layah groaned and hunched over her cereal bowl.

If she was going to have her thirteenth birthday in the middle of nowhere, she'd rather just ignore it.

'But Layah, how are you feeling?' said Mum. 'After your sleepwalking last night.'

'I think I'm all right,' said Layah. 'It was just a bit . . . creepy.'

Her mum's brow furrowed and Izzie lowered her book.

'It doesn't matter!' Layah added breezily. 'Dad says too much cheese gives you bad dreams. It must have been all those cheesy nibbles we had last night. Anyway, what are we doing today?' She looked at her mum. 'Maybe we could all go out for scones?'

But her mum wasn't listening; she was busy putting away the cereal boxes. Layah felt a swell of annoyance.

'Yes, you go to the village,' said Mum vaguely, 'I've

got a couple of chores to do here first then we're meeting Henry and his son at the Boating Centre at two.'

'Do we have to?'

Layah rolled her eyes at Izzie, who grimaced in agreement.

'Henry is one of my oldest school friends, Layah. He didn't need to lend us this cottage,' chided Mum, 'and all I ask from you is a *teaspoon* of politeness.'

'Does cake count as lunch?' interrupted Izzie.

'Yes, fine!' said Mum distractedly. 'But make sure you eat an apple later. Layah, here you go.'

Her mum passed Layah a twenty-pound note and her fingers brushed against the amber necklace. Izzie was wearing her necklace too, the pendant glinting like a drop of swirling sunset.

'It's lovely that you're still wearing them,' said Mum softly.

'Of course.' Layah frowned. 'We'll always wear them.'

Her mum touched it gently before straightening up. 'Perfect! Now off you go!' she said, cheery once more. 'You should be outside having fun.'

Layah wished she wouldn't pretend. Why couldn't her mum just admit it? Admit that the only reason they'd left in such a hurry was because she was running away from her marriage. Layah didn't know if their family would ever get back to normal again.

The hazy rain cut through the sunlight as Layah and Izzie strode down the winding road which led to the village of Lowesdale. The sprawling lake glittered below them and ahead the craggy mountain face of the Lowesdale Giant stood up bold against the sky. This was their fourth day of being chucked out of the cottage. Their mum hadn't invited them on her long walks – 'I just want to clear my head,' she'd protested, 'you'd be bored!' – but had instructed them to explore the village and always stick together. Layah knew there was no point complaining and she couldn't let Izzie go out on her own.

'Layah, when are we going home?' said Izzie, as soon as Rook Cottage was out of sight behind them. 'We'll be back before school starts, right?'

Layah kicked a pebble into the ditch but said nothing.

'If we're staying until your birthday, I might miss the Year Seven induction day!' Izzie said, hurrying to keep pace with Layah. 'If I miss it, I won't know where anything is – what if I don't get my library pass?'

Layah snorted. Izzie had avoided the bullies in primary school, but secondary school would be different. Teenagers noticed things. Layah knew they didn't like you to be different. She felt a hot lump in her throat at the thought of the mouthy boys in her year laughing at Izzie's odd socks or her green rucksack.

'And I was going to buy my new schoolbooks with Dad,' continued Izzie, 'I don't want to miss that.'

'Get used to it,' muttered Layah.

She ripped off a leaf from the hedgerow and started tearing it into pieces, a knot of annoyance tightening inside her.

'But Dad's coming to join us?' pressed Izzie. 'He's still coming, isn't he, Layah?'

'That's it!' Layah snapped. 'Enough with the stupid questions!'

She marched ahead, tugging up her jacket collar and crossing her arms across her chest.

The truth was, they had barely heard from their dad since he'd gone to the conference in Denmark. Yet their mum was still acting like they were on a jolly holiday and everything was fine! Layah heard Izzie's footsteps flopping behind her and felt a rush of guilt. She shouldn't have shouted. It wasn't Izzie's fault that she was an oblivious bookworm. Layah crunched around another bend in the lane, glaring at the soggy scenery until she saw something which made her stumble to a stop.

Layah turned as Izzie came around the corner, looking at her shoes.

'Izzie, don't look behind me. Close your eyes! Just don't look at the hedge.'

'What is it?' cried Izzie, as Layah threw out an arm to shield her view.

'It's an animal. It's dead. Just don't look at it.'

Izzie clamped her eyes shut and she felt her way down the road, Layah's hand tight on her arm. Layah wished she too could look away, wished she could un-see it, but it was impossible. The creature was tangled in the thorns of the hedge – a dash of brown disturbing the dark green leaves, its wings outstretched as if frozen mid-flight. There was a dark stain on its fluffy chest.

'What animal?' asked Izzie.

'A bird.'

Izzie shuddered and quickened her pace.

'It's OK,' said Layah, 'we're passing it. Just round this bend.'

Layah tore her eyes away from the poor creature. It felt cruel to leave it there, strung up like a puppet, but she couldn't bear the thought of approaching it. When they reached the bridge into the village, Layah let go of Izzie's arm. Izzie looked up at her, white-faced.

'Was it hit by a car?' whispered Izzie.

'I don't think so. I think it must have been killed by a fox or something.'

Izzie looked a little pale.

'Hey, let's go to the Boat Café,' said Layah, trying to sound cheerful. 'I think the next cake we need to try is peanut-butter fudge. You in?'

Izzie gave a small smile, which Layah returned. Without looking back, the two sisters hurried towards the lake.

Lowesdale Village was an in-between place, half-forgotten amongst the rolling fells of the Lakes. Ramblers, country cyclists and the occasional holidaying family stopped off in Lowesdale on their way somewhere else. The village high street boasted a grocer, bookshop, the Old Singer Tea Room and a post office selling doorstops shaped like dogs, and biscuits shaped like sheep.

At the edge of Lowesdale Lake there was a café which looked out over the water and the sleepy Boating Centre, which had more boats than customers. The Boat Café advertised an eccentric selection of cakes and Izzie had set them the challenge of sampling the whole menu. Their top favourites so far had included marmalade pavlova, sherbet and raspberry sponge and upside-down coconut cake.

Layah headed for the table by the window while

Izzie veered towards the counter. Layah gazed out at the bobbing boats. She couldn't get rid of the image of the little bird in the hedge. Those bright eyes in that tiny head were scorched into her mind's eye.

Izzie clattered back to the table with a giant slab of peanut-butter fudge cake and two forks. Izzie reached towards her rucksack for her book but then she paused, closed it again, and looked up at Layah.

'Why would a fox leave a bird in the hedge?' said Izzie slowly. 'Why wouldn't it just eat it?'

'I don't know . . .' Layah hesitated then added, 'but let's not talk about it. I don't want to upset you.'

In truth, Layah was still feeling a little queasy herself.

'I'm fine, honestly, Layah. It was just a bit of a shock.'

'Come on, let's eat!' Layah took a mouthful of cake. 'I reckon the raspberry sponge has got competition!'

Izzie was soon judging the new cake from squishiness to sweetness, and Layah watched her intently. A few years ago, even mentioning a dead animal would have brought Izzie close to tears. But she was eleven now, Layah kept forgetting that. It was as if her younger sister was catching up with her. The thought made Layah feel slightly less alone.

Izzie was just considering asking for chocolate sauce

when Layah noticed that the light had faded. The coloured flags on the boats seemed dulled and the gnawing of the waves had gone silent. A shadow crept over Lowesdale.

Then Layah heard the whistling. A piercing, unworldly tune. Her breath caught in her throat. She looked back at Izzie, who was blabbing away as if nothing had happened, but Layah definitely heard something.

And then she saw her.

The woman from her nightmare was standing in the entrance of the Boat Café. She was staring at Layah. Her face, hollow and chewed with age, was contorted with a smile. Her eyes were not as huge, nor as luminously yellow, as they had been the night before, but there was a lemon tinge to them which made Layah's skin crawl. They stared at each other. Then the woman whirled away, darting out of the door.

'Layah! What's wrong?'

Layah had pushed back the table and was stumbling through the forest of chairs towards the door. She heard Izzie call again but didn't look round.

Layah burst out of the café and looked up the street. She could see the old woman weaving through a straggle of local farmers. Layah hesitated for a second – Izzie was still calling her from inside the café – then

16

sprinted off, but the woman was too far ahead and moving extraordinarily fast, her white hair billowing out behind her. Layah saw a final flash of those yellow eyes as the woman disappeared down a side street.

Layah, panting, reached the corner and dashed round it. The street was empty. She jogged past a row of sleepy cottages; a striped cat watched her from a window, but there was no sign of the woman. She stumbled to a walk and finally stopped. The street had opened up on to a main road out into the countryside. She was all alone.

Layah looked up and saw a looming stone building with iron railings penning in a courtyard beyond. Skylarks quarrelled on the rooftop and the windows were blank and lifeless. A sign hung on the gate:

## LOWESDALE SCHOOL FOR YOUNG LADIES

A silver sports car screeched past, horn blaring, and Layah tripped backwards out of the road. She gazed across the street, still hypnotised by the school.

'Layah! Layah!' Izzie was charging towards her, the remains of the cake clutched in a napkin. 'Layah, what's going on?'

'It wasn't a dream,' Layah cried, 'it was the woman.

Didn't you see her? She was at the café – long white hair and those yellow eyes!'

'What woman?' Izzie's eyes were round.

'Last night I had this dream. I thought I'd dreamed that I saw a woman in the garden but I've just seen her. She's real! Only she wasn't a normal person— No! What am I saying?' Layah was struggling to keep up with her racing thoughts. 'No, of course she was a normal person!'

'You saw a woman in the garden?' said Izzie shakily. 'Who was she? What did she want?'

'I don't know,' replied Layah, 'but I need to find out.'

Layah looked up at the windows of Lowesdale School; the place seemed deserted. Had the woman meant for Layah to follow her here? She had no idea. Questions were pinging around her head. But one fact had screwed itself into Layah's mind: she hadn't been sleepwalking. She hadn't been dreaming. Her mum had lied to her.

The beam of the dying moon winked off the window, as the girl eased up the pane and slipped over the sill. She stumbled as her bare feet landed on cold stone. She stiffened for a second but the patter of the rain outside had masked her movements. Her eyes traced the room, shrouded in creeping shadows. Her heart beat furiously, but it was not the darkness she feared. She was used to darkness.

The girl licked her fingers; she could still taste that sweet, sticky something she had taken from the shop. The owner would never suspect a break-in. She had ways of making things look natural. Anything – a sudden gust of wind or a flailing branch – could have caused the window to jerk open. Chocolate: that was what had been written on the jar. She'd remember that.

The girl looked across the room. There was a door at the other end, half camouflaged in the thick blackness. She took a step forward. Stealth is a game of patience. She moved without sound; the drum of her heart and murmur of the rain trembled in her ears. One more step. The door loomed into view; she reached for the handle but – too late!

A hand shot out of the darkness and clamped her wrist like a vice. The girl was pulled, half thrown, back into the room and hit the floor with a crack. She twisted, cringing up at the face which reared above her.

'No one saw me,' stammered the girl, 'no one will know! I just wanted to see . . .'

'Spare me the tears, you ungrateful girl!' spat the Other. 'You know our rules! You dare to venture outside without permission, when you know what you could be risking!'

The girl could only babble in response. The Other dropped her wrist in disgust.

'Look at you, fool. Where is your pride? Stand up and face me, instead of sniffling and whining.'

The girl scrambled to her feet, rolling back her shoulders and raising her chin. The Other observed her through narrowed eyes.

'You are certain you were not seen?'

'Yes – yes, of course,' whispered the girl, 'I can be fast.'

There was an icy pause.

'If that is the case, then I am impressed. Indeed,

you are improving in your studies,' the Other said. 'Perhaps you are ready for greater challenges. The timing is right, after all.'

The girl's eyes darted up. 'Yes. Yes, I'm ready to prove myself!'

'We shall see,' said the Other. 'For now, go to your room and do not leave it until I call you. Know that if you ever disobey me again there will be consequences.'

The words embedded themselves like spikes in the silence. The girl stood her ground.

'I shall not disappoint you.'

The girl looked up, her neck arching, her yellow eyes blazing in the solemn gloom.

# Chapter Three

Layah was still wired from her chase with the strange woman. As she and Izzie hurried along the lakeside, towards the Boating Centre, Layah tried searching the school on her mobile but the signal was – as usual – terrible. Layah was in no mood to go canoeing. She needed to process what had just happened and what it all meant. And she needed to talk to her mum.

Layah was trying to remember exactly what had happened the night before. Had there been panic in her mum's face when Layah had mentioned the whistling? Her mum had asked, 'What did she look like?' but had that been before or after Layah had said it was a woman? Had Mum deliberately lied to Layah about the sleepwalking? Or had she made a mistake?

As they reached the boats, Layah spotted her mum talking to a man with thick blonde hair.

'Mum! I need to talk to you!' Layah began as soon

as they were within earshot.

'Layah, not now.' Their mum turned to the man beside her. 'Layah, Izzie, I'd like you to meet my old friend, Henry. He went to school with your dad in London, you know. He hasn't seen you since you were tiny!'

Henry sauntered forward. He had the air of a politician and the haircut of a man who paid for perfection. As his eyes fell on her, Layah felt like he was pricing her up.

'Hi, girls, ready for a canoe-a-roo?' Henry smirked.

Layah and Izzie regarded him with identical stony expressions.

'The girls and I want to say thanks, again,' Mum gushed, 'for putting us up in Rook Cottage. It's beautiful.'

'It's got good bones, Ren, I'll give you that!' he drawled. 'Still got most of the old Westwood family furniture. But it's a draughty old place. You should have taken my spare rooms in the Manor. The offer's still there. I know you'd brighten up the place.'

'We're perfectly fine in the cottage, just the three of us.' She laughed, wafting away his compliment.

Henry's eyes swivelled back to Layah and Izzie. 'So how are you liking the Lakes, girls?'

'It rains a lot,' said Layah shortly.

'They've got Kosmatka's love of nature, have they, Ren? Take after the mad Russian professor, then?' Henry barked a laugh.

'Dad's not a professor,' said Izzie waspishly, 'he's a zoological research scientist, actually. And he's Polish, not Russian.'

Henry looked temporarily aghast as if a hamster had just nipped him on the finger. Layah bit back her grin with difficulty.

'Henry has just got back from Rome.' Their mum interrupted the awkward moment.

'Visiting my little brother, Jonny.' Henry nodded. 'Of course, I came back early when I knew Ren was going to take the cottage. Always happy to ride to the rescue!'

Henry's self-satisfied smirk made Layah want to kick dirt on his white trousers.

'Ah, James! Got the wetsuits?' Henry boomed over their heads.

'Wetsuits?' Layah hissed to her mum. 'I'm not wearing a wetsuit – you know, they're like rubber onesies! This is cruelty to kids!'

Her mum gave a warning frown and Layah turned to see who Henry was hailing. Her grimace met a slim, athletic boy with light brown skin and green eyes. He looked around the same age as her, but swaggered with a confidence ahead of his years. He had the unmistakable attitude of a Westwood.

'Here's your rubber onesie,' he said, flopping a wetsuit into her arms. 'I doubt they're destined for the catwalk, but hey, you can always wear your regular swimsuit. I'm sure some minor leg spasms and frostbite is nothing compared to committing a fashion felony!'

The boy was grinning at her but Layah scowled.

'Come on, girls, let's go to the changing rooms, shall we?' called Mum, linking Izzie's arm in hers and marching away.

Layah made to follow too but the boy fell into step beside her.

'James,' he said, holding out a hand, 'James Westwood. I'm guessing you're Layah.'

Layah kept her arms crossed and glowered as she crunched over the shingle.

'Why come canoeing if you don't like the outfit?' he said, hurrying to keep up.

'I'm here with my mum,' said Layah testily. 'We're on holiday.'

'Oh, right! Bit of a last-minute holiday, wasn't it? I thought you might be looking for a new school.'

She stared at him; his green eyes sparkled.

'What do you mean?'

'Father and I saw you looking at Lowesdale Girls just now. Poor choice, if you ask me. Hideous uniforms!'

'Do you go to school here?' asked Layah, curious despite herself.

'No, my father ships me out to a school more befitting the Westwood family name – top hats, rice pudding, high expectations – you get the picture.' He waved the topic away. 'But you know Lowesdale Girls is supposed to be haunted?'

Layah didn't answer, but her heart lurched uncomfortably.

'Oh yeah,' James continued, 'it's full of the ghosts of dead teachers and murdered students. But I guess a tough non-wetsuit-wearing person like you wouldn't listen to village gossip.'

'What kind of gossip?'

James grinned, clearly enjoying having an audience.

'Lowesdale is full of ghost stories and monster myths.' He smiled. 'You never heard of the Lowesdale Stranger? Villagers say the Stranger lives in the forest on the Giant, and steals down to the village at night to feast on sheep and children out of bed!'

'Is the Lowesdale Stranger a man or a woman?'

James laughed and Layah suddenly felt foolish.

'The child-eating monster can be whatever you want it to be.' James flicked his dark fringe out of his eyes. 'Don't tell me you believe those kind of made-up stories?'

'Of course not.' Layah scowled fiercely. 'My babcia taught me that people make up stories to explain things or teach kids a lesson.'

'Or to scare people.' James grinned, his eyes glinting. 'Just admit you're a little scared.'

'No, I'm not! I'm not scared of made-up stories or arrogant rich boys.'

'Ouch!' He laughed. 'Can't argue with that – but I'm actually a *countryside* arrogant rich boy – we're the most dangerous variety.'

Layah bit back a grin.

'So is your mum usually this spontaneous?' he asked. 'One call from her and my father's cancelling half our holiday. Why are you really here?'

They had reached the door of the ladies' changing rooms and she spun to face him.

'Would you kindly butt out of my family's private life?'

James's smile wavered. A crowd of bickering seagulls paused to watch them.

'Sorry – I was just joking around. We don't get many other kids here and I reckoned you could do with a friend – I mean, a friendly Lowesdale guide.' He gave a mock bow.

'I don't need any friends,' muttered Layah, 'I'm fine.'

She turned and pushed into the changing room, her face hot. Even an outsider like James Westwood had recognised the strangeness of her mum's behaviour. Were the cracks in her family that obvious?

Fifteen minutes of hopping, stumbling and cursing later, Layah, Izzie and their mum left the changing rooms, fully wetsuited. Layah still hadn't found a moment to talk to her mum but as soon as they emerged, they saw Henry and James standing by two canoes in the water. Layah was irritated to notice that even in a wetsuit James still looked cool, whereas Layah felt like she was wearing a baggy skinsuit.

'We've got a big'un and a little'un,' Henry boomed. 'We'll have the kids in one and the adults in the other. James, take the Avery route and we'll go straight.'

'Maybe me, Mum and Izzie can go in the big one?' said Layah quickly. 'We haven't done it before.'

'Layah, can you please just do this – for me!' Mum whispered, before calling to Henry, 'Wonderful! It'll be an adventure.'

After they had all strapped on lifejackets and Layah

had disentangled Izzie's hair from one of the paddles, the two canoes pushed off, side by side. Henry and their mum soon glided off into the centre of Lowesdale Lake, but James pointed their boat around the perimeter. Paddling had a hypnotic tempo and Layah found her mind drifting. Why had James told her about this Lowesdale Stranger and the gossip about the school being haunted? Layah knew he was just teasing her but there was certainly something weird going on. Perhaps the woman was a teacher at the school. But that still wouldn't explain what she was doing poking around their garden in the middle of the night, or why her mum had lied about the sleepwalking.

Layah stared out over the rippling lake, the waves winking like so many dancing mirrors. Layah's mum had always been the sun around which her daughters had orbited but now she was deliberately keeping them in the dark.

'Layah! You're supposed to be paddling!' called Izzie from behind her.

James glanced back at her and Layah hastily dug her paddle into the water.

'Keep a steady pace,' said James calmly, 'one on each side. One. Two. One—'

'All right! We can count!' retorted Layah.

Looking behind them, she realised they were alone. Henry and their mum were out of sight behind the bend in the lake and the village too had vanished.

'What's that island?' Izzie called, pointing across the water.

Layah looked up. It was like a large hill rising out of the lake, spread with trees and shrubbery.

'Avery Island,' said James, twisting round. 'Been in the family for a couple of hundred years.'

'What?' Layah scoffed. 'You own an island?'

'Yeah, why not?' He shrugged.

'That's cool!' marvelled Izzie.

'You own an *island*?' Layah repeated. 'What do you do with it?'

'Not much. It's just an island. And it doesn't have any secret helicopter pads or underwater lairs, if that's what you're thinking. Want to take a closer look?'

Layah squinted across the water. There were birds, like smudges of ink in the sky, drifting above the island. Goosebumps rolled down her spine and the hairs on her arms stood on end. It wasn't just the birds, there was something else, too . . . an eerie darkness seemed to shroud the island. The clouds had turned charcoal-grey and the lake seemed black beneath it.

As Layah watched, the birds began clustering

together to form a fluttering mass which arced in the sky and began to soar towards the canoe, their cawing voices echoing in a strange song. Layah, Izzie and James craned their necks as the birds paused, high above them, and began to circle, like vultures assessing a corpse.

'Let's go back to shore,' said Layah. 'We need to go back! Now!'

'It's just a thing birds do,' reassured James, 'it's called a murmuration. It's perfectly normal.' But his voice was dry as he eyed the swirling birds.

'I agree with Layah,' said Izzie, 'I think we should go back.'

'OK. Let's turn this canoe around.' James shrugged but Layah sensed he was relieved. He managed to reassert his arrogant ease when he added: 'And Layah, try not to splash me so much this time.'

Layah couldn't think of anything to respond. Her heart was pounding and she didn't dare look back at the birds as the canoe forged through the waves, but she could feel their hundreds of eyes watching and waiting.

# Chapter Four

Henry drove them back to Rook Cottage, their mum in the passenger seat and Layah and Izzie in the back with James. The sun was melting into the horizon and the air was sweet with stale rain.

James plugged in his headphones and stared out of the window as his father droned on in time to the engine. Layah couldn't blame him. She felt like she had sat through double science when the car finally bumped down the track to the cottage. The sisters tumbled out, leaving their mum to thank Henry alone.

Layah closed the front door behind Izzie. As she kicked off her Doc Martens, she noticed a bolt at the bottom of the door. The screws were lopsided; clearly a rushed job. She went to look at the back door in the kitchen – another new bolt. Izzie padded in behind her. The glare of the kitchen light was already making mirrors of the windows. The garden beyond was growing dark.

'Did you notice . . . were these bolts here before?' asked Layah.

'No,' said Izzie, 'there's a packet in the bin. Mum must have done them while we were out today.'

'But why?'

Before Izzie could answer, the front door slammed. Both girls turned as their mum wandered into the kitchen.

'Who's up for pancakes?' She clapped her hands together.

'Mum, what are these new bolts?' asked Layah. 'Are you locking us in? Or keeping someone out?'

Both sisters examined their mum. Her fingers fumbled to readjust her hair clip.

'Don't be silly, Layah. They've always been there,' she said, marching over to the mixing bowl. 'Henry has invited us to visit a hotel he's just bought. It's in Newbeck, next Wednesday. Now I know it's your birthday, Layah, so let me know if you'd rather not but—'

'Mum! Are you kidding? Celebrate my birthday with *Henry*?! Honestly, how can you stand him?' exploded Layah. 'He's arrogant and annoying and—'

'He doesn't know the difference between a professor and a zoological research scientist,' added Izzie.

'He is *so* not your kind of person,' continued Layah. 'Do you even like him? Why—'

Their mum whirled to face them, wooden spoon in hand.

'Oh, girls! I know Henry seemed a little . . . full of himself but he's doing us a huge favour! He's letting us stay here, for nothing.'

'So, it's just about the cottage then?'

'Layah! If you stop playing the stroppy daughter, I will stop acting the evil mother,' berated Mum, her face pink. 'It's not my fault your dad wasn't at home to look after you – I mean . . .'

Layah felt like someone had pulled the floor away.

'You don't even want us here?' Layah breathed.

'That's not what I said,' Mum huffed, grabbing the bowl and upturning a bag of flour.

'You wanted to get away from us!' said Layah. 'Now Babcia's died, we don't need to pretend to be a happy family any more?'

'Layah, you're being ridiculous! I didn't mean—'

'I saw the woman again today.' Layah took a shaky breath. 'She's real. She led me to Lowesdale School.'

Their mum froze, wooden spoon aloft. Izzie's eyes were zipping back and forth between them.

'You were sleepwalking,' said Mum firmly. 'It was just a dream.'

'I wasn't sleepwalking and it wasn't a dream, and you know it!' said Layah, her voice rising, that knot of frustration tugging inside her chest. 'Who is she, Mum? Why was she watching us? I know you know something.'

There was a flicker and – without warning – the lights went out and the kitchen was doused in sudden gloom.

Layah bolted to the switch and twisted it but the light was dead. The whole house was in darkness. A hand clasped Layah's arm and she gasped.

'What's happened!' said Izzie, her eyes reflecting shadows.

'Oh, blast! The fuse is gone!' came Mum's voice. 'Give me a moment. I'll call Henry.'

They stood in the black, listening to the ringing mobile. Layah's heart was knocking against her ribs. She was very aware of the silence outside the windows. The isolation of the cottage. It was so far down the private track that it was impossible for anyone to see or hear them from the road.

'Henry! Yes. Hi. It's Ren. You just got home?'

Layah could tell her mum was trying to sound calm. The house creaked around them.

'We've had a little trouble. The lights have gone out,' said Mum, airily. 'Just tell me where the fuse box is, and I can—'

*THUD!*

Something heavy hit the front door. Layah tensed, waiting for it to strike again; Izzie was clutching Layah's sleeve. There was something outside.

'Henry, I'll just call you back!' Mum stammered. 'I'll . . . we can handle it.'

She cut the call and edged out of the kitchen and across the living room. Layah followed; her body was prickling with fear. Whatever had made that noise might still be out there waiting to strike again.

Her mum held up the light of her phone; the bluish beam swung across the room. The new bolts on the front door winked in the light. Slowly, their mum moved forward, her hand fumbling for the latch.

'Girls, don't move.' Their mum flung open the door and let out a sharp cry. 'Oh my goodness!'

Layah rushed to the doorway. It was framed in the light from the phone, bent and lifeless upon the horsehair mat. Another dead bird. It had been dead before it hit the door.

Layah reeled back into the house.

'Don't look—' Layah began but it was too late.

Izzie was staring down at the creature, stiff with fear. Layah swore and dragged her sister back inside.

'Go into the kitchen,' commanded Mum. 'I'll deal with this.'

Layah and Izzie dropped into chairs at the table, both looking out at the shifting garden. A storm was simmering as they listened to their mum walking around the outside. Layah's knees were jittering under the table but Izzie was hypnotically still.

'Was that like the bird from the road?' whispered Izzie.

'Yeah.' Layah swallowed. 'And Iz, I – I think they were meant for us.'

The lights burst on again and Layah jumped.

'I've fixed the fuse,' Mum announced, walking in and heading swiftly towards the kettle. 'What we need now is a good cup of mint tea.'

'Mum, that's the second dead bird we've seen,' said Layah, standing up. 'Someone killed them. At least it looks like that. Why are these things happening?'

Her mum turned to face Layah; her eyes were over-bright.

'Layah, don't panic!' Mum said. 'They can't hurt us – I mean . . .'

'Who?' demanded Layah. 'The woman? Is she dangerous? Mum? What do you mean "they"?'

'They? No, that's not what I said. There's nothing to be afraid of.' Her voice cracked. 'I've got everything under—'

'When can we go home?' said Izzie, looking up from the table.

'I don't know. I just need some more time,' sighed Mum. 'I'll get the pancakes on. There's nothing to worry about.'

'I think I'm going to read upstairs,' muttered Izzie, 'I'm not hungry.'

Izzie slipped out of the room. Pity rolled over Layah as she saw the miserable expression on her mum's face.

'Layah, I know there has been a lot of change recently. I know the stuff between me and your dad has made you upset,' said Mum, 'but I need you to trust me.'

'How can we trust you when you won't tell us anything?' said Layah, retreating towards the door.

Layah knew she was being harsh but she couldn't help it. She wished she knew exactly what to say to make her mum open up – to unlock this wall between them.

Babcia would have known what to do. Layah wished

she could talk to her. She wished she was with them. Babcia would have sat them down at her kitchen table with a slab of hazelnut *tort*, and fixed them all with a hard stare: 'Talk! Listen! And eat!' She always knew how to solve any family argument. Layah wished she had her patience.

But there was no point talking to her mum if all she did was lie. If her mum wouldn't tell them what was going on, Layah would have to find out herself.

The heavens had cracked and black rain was falling through the night. Droplets drummed the leaves above them as the girl followed the Other deeper into the forest.

'Quickly now!' the Other commanded. 'You have done well tonight – your skills are improving – but it would not do for the sun to catch us.'

The girl stumbled over a root, her bare toes squishing into the wet mud. She hastened to the Other's side, her yellow eyes scanning the forest. The birds were watching them. The girl could sense their small, bright eyes tracking their every step – the hunched blackbirds in the branches, the shifty starlings in the thicket and the owl peering down from the tallest tree. The birds were afraid of them, the girl knew it.

And then, keen as a magpie, she spotted something in the dirt.

'What's that?' said the girl, swooping to retrieve it.

'Keep your voice down,' hissed the Other.

The girl rose with the object in her hand. It was a

bracelet. A gold band which glinted in the moonlight. It had dropped on to the path. Forgotten in the forest.

'Well?' prompted the Other, arms crossed. 'Your lessons are never over, so tell me: what can we learn from it?'

The girl turned the bracelet over in her hands.

'The gold is real,' she said slowly, 'and it's small.' She slipped it on to her wrist. 'It must have been a present – for a child. There's an engraving . . . a name. There's no damage, the mud rubs off easily, so it can't have been here for long.'

The Other glared around them – the birds quivered and even the trees seemed to shiver.

'Can I keep it?'

'Keep it?' sneered the Other. 'Whatever for? We do not need trinkets.'

The girl rotated the bracelet on her wrist, her mouth dry.

'I thought it might be nice.'

'Nice! Nice?' The Other strode towards her and the rain started to fall more frantically. 'Objects have one use for us: they give us information on our foe – our prey. On rare occasions, so the Teachings tell us, we may use objects to hold secrets and power.'

'But jewellery and precious things, they can tell people's stories.' The girl frowned. 'I just wanted something special.'

The Other caught her by the wrist and the girl cried out in pain – the birds began to flutter agitatedly.

'Do not contradict me!' snarled the Other, her teeth bared. 'You are just a child! I know the Teachings! I know what is right for you!'

'Y – yes,' stammered the girl.

The Other shook her off and the girl fell on to the wet ground.

'Special objects are sentimental. Sentiment is emotional,' said the Other. 'Emotion is weak and we must reject it. As we must reject all human things! We are not like them.'

The girl clambered to her feet. The light in her eyes dimmed.

'I know what we are,' she murmured, head hanging.

The Other was not watching her any more. Her attention had been caught by something in the shadow of a tree. The Other's eyes glistened as she sniffed the air.

'Now, what have we here?'

She advanced and the girl followed. A wicker box was nestled in the tree's roots. The Other opened the lid to reveal several packets of biscuits.

'What is this?' The Other's voice was deadly.

'There's a note,' said the girl. 'It says: for the stranger on the mountain. *Does it mean—*'

'It is rare for someone to travel this far into the forest,' the Other muttered. 'We must take this as a sign. Double our protections. The curiosity of the villagers will not be our downfall.'

The Other snatched the note and stomped it into the dirt. She attacked the biscuits next, cracking and crumbling them into the mud.

The Other swept away between the trees.

'Come!' she hissed to the girl. 'We must go! The villagers must be taught a lesson in fear. We must add to our protections! Leave the bracelet – I want no more argument!'

The girl dropped the bracelet at her feet.

They set off again, rustling through the shadows. Only once did the girl glance back. Her eyes found the bracelet and she watched as a sparrow darted down to snatch it from the forest floor. The girl gave a secret smile.

# CHAPTER FIVE

The village bookshop was a lopsided building in the centre of Lowesdale. Izzie had done a little dance when she'd first seen it. Inside, spindly shelves snaked through the shop, blocking out the light and plunging the place into never-ending twilight. Layah left Izzie perched in her favourite corner (Fantasy Adventure) and followed the maze of books to the front of the shop. If it hadn't been for Izzie's apparent life-or-death urgency to buy a new book, Layah doubted their mum would have let them leave the cottage. Despite her assurances that everything was 'perfectly fine', their mum seemed worried. A tight frown had been plastered to her face all day. She made Layah promise not to leave Izzie's side, and to be back before dark.

Layah found the shelf labelled Ancient History, and ran a finger down the spines, searching. Whenever she was in a bookshop, Layah always looked for the same book. She found it at the end of the row: *Tales from*

44

*Ancient Poland: Songs of Kings and Monsters* by Professor Ana Kosmatka. Layah's babcia. She had been a professor of ancient history at the university in Krakow, discovering lost poems and stories about quest-hungry warriors, evil beasts and magic eagles, written in strange, forgotten languages which she translated. These stories, Babcia explained, showed how people used to see the world. Babcia had given her last talk at the university only a week before she died. Layah always thought she'd like to be like her when she grew up: a historian, searching for truth in old tales.

The musty smell of the bookshop reminded her of Babcia's study. When Layah was little she would sit on a pile of books and watch Babcia translating her latest discovery, poring over parchments. Occasionally, Babcia would look over her purple glasses at six-year-old Layah: 'What do you think this word is?' she'd ask. 'Spear or sword? After your father teaches you Polish, I will teach you the forgotten languages – Ancient Slavic and Old Polish!'

Their dad never did have time to teach them Polish, and Layah and Izzie only knew a handful of words, one of which was '*ogórki*', which meant 'pickled cucumber'.

The rumble of an engine made Layah look up. A red motorbike – or perhaps it was a scooter – was rolling up outside the bookshop, sunlight glinting off the paintwork. The rider pulled off his helmet: it was James Westwood.

'Oh, of course he's got a stupid, expensive bike,' Layah mumbled to herself. It was the least she'd expected from a fourteen-year-old boy whose family owned an island.

A dog came hurtling out of the post office, barking furiously. James flapped it away, looking up and down the street. He turned in his seat to face the bookshop and Layah ducked out of sight.

There was a rumble and she saw the scooter buzzing off towards the lake, the dog yapping at its fumes.

Layah wondered why James was hanging around the village on his own. Didn't he have any other snotty friends to hang out with? But then Layah remembered James went to boarding school, so he might not have any friends in Lowesdale. Her sympathy for him ended when she remembered how he'd teased her about the ghost stories. The stuff he'd said about the school was still bugging her. She didn't believe it was haunted but there was definitely something weird about it. Layah needed action. She needed answers and she wasn't going to find them in this dingy bookshop.

Babcia had once travelled – by plane, train and

Highland cow – all the way from Poland to the Isle of Mull in Scotland, pursuing the missing page of a lost poem. 'I might be a woman of learning,' Babcia remarked to Layah, 'but sometimes the best lessons come from adventures – going outside, getting lost, asking questions and finding answers!' Six-year-old Layah had beamed at the thought, picturing herself as Babcia's assistant, travelling to far-off places together. She pushed open the bookshop door.

'Layah! Wait!' Izzie had scrambled up from her nest of books. 'Where are you going?'

'I need to do something,' said Layah, 'just stay here.'

Layah clanged the door shut before waiting for an answer and strode off down the road. Undeterred, Izzie came rocketing after her.

'Iz! Just go wait in the bookshop,' Layah protested.

'Are you going to the school?' said Izzie excitedly. 'Are you going to find out who the woman is?'

'Yes – but I can do it alone. Just go back to your books.'

'No, Layah, I'm coming too,' Izzie demanded, crossing her arms in very Layah-like gesture.

'Fine, but don't tell Mum,' conceded Layah, and they set off together.

Lowesdale School cut a bleak outline against the pastel

blue sky. The stone walls and the arched windows made the place look more like a prison than a school. Layah paced up and down the gate, squinting through the rails. The building looked just as deserted as the day before – not a shadow moved in the courtyard.

Izzie loitered at Layah's shoulder. 'Something's up with Mum,' said Izzie at last.

'Yep. Full marks, Sherlock,' Layah responded drily.

'Did you notice her stretching the washing line across the back lawn?' Izzie went on. 'Like she was creating some kind of tripwire. Who do you think threw the bird at the door?'

'I reckon Mum knows,' said Layah, 'but she's not going to tell us.'

Last night, their mum had let slip the existence of a 'they'. Did she mean the woman or was there someone else?

'But why?' pressed Izzie. 'Did they want to scare us? Who was bird-killer's target? What was their motivation?'

Layah blinked at her sister; she'd never heard Izzie talk so seriously about something other than a book. She was suddenly deeply grateful to have her there.

'Well,' said Layah slowly, 'Mum is the obvious choice.'

'It could be gang-related!' Izzie exclaimed. 'The dead

LONDON BOROUGH OF
RICHMOND UPON THAMES

## Hampton Hill Library
68 High Street, Hampton Hill, TW12 1NY

Account: \*\*\*\*\*\*\*4064

---

### The bird singers
Due date. 01/06/22

---

Total items borrowed: 1

---

11/05/22 2:24 PM

birds could be a warning! Gangsters are always sending each other dead horse heads!'

'Gross!' Layah squirmed. 'Iz, Mum's not part of a gang! It's not like she looks after government secrets or anything – she works in a gallery!'

She gazed back at the school. What was the bird-killer hoping to achieve?

'Layah?' said Izzie cautiously. 'When we were here yesterday you said . . . you said the woman wasn't a normal person. What did you mean?'

'Oh, I was just being dramatic,' said Layah quickly.

'It just sounded like you meant she wasn't quite . . . *human*. And those birds yesterday, near Avery Island, the way they circled us, it was so strange.'

'Of course she's human! You're just going to scare yourself if you start talking like that,' protested Layah, but a cold chill was spreading through her at Izzie's words.

Layah glanced up the crooked lane which led to the village. The nearest cottages had frilly curtains hiding any inquisitive neighbours from view. Layah turned back to the school, her mind made up.

'That woman brought me to the school for a reason. The question is – how do I get inside?'

'Look! That window,' called Izzie, squishing her face

between the rails.

Layah spotted it too – one of the windows on the ground floor had been left slightly open.

'All right!' commanded Layah, placing a foot on the railings. 'You stay here and I'll be back in a minute. Give me a push up.'

Layah heaved herself over the railings and landed in a rose bush on the other side. She staggered up and looked around. Maybe it was her imagination, but it seemed darker on this side of the gate. Thick shadows hung around the school. Layah didn't let herself think the word 'ghost' but it was certainly ghostly.

Glancing from side to side, she jogged across the courtyard to the half-open window. There was an elm tree beside the school, with strange black wind chimes jangling in the branches. Layah placed her hands on the window and after some jiggling, the frame jerked upwards. She vaulted over the sill and landed on the floor with an 'oof'. Layah looked up. This school wasn't anything like her school back home, which was all modern glass and metal. The corridor was lined with oak panels and tasselled lamps swung from the ceiling; there were glass cabinets full of gold trophies. The air smelt of mothballs and wood polish.

'Is anyone here?' echoed a voice.

Layah yelped, turning to see Izzie tumble over the window frame and crash to the floor.

'I told you to stay outside,' said Layah, pulling Izzie to her feet and dusting her down.

'Wow . . .'

Izzie stepped forward, running her hand over the wood-panelled walls. Layah followed stealthily.

Despite its decrepit overcoat, the school was definitely still in use. They passed noticeboards with posters and leaflets for school clubs.

Izzie pinched Layah's elbow. 'Layah! Did you hear that?'

'What was—'

*Tap-tap. Tap-tap.*

It was the unmistakable sound of footsteps on the tiled floor. Layah looked back at the open window – it was too far to make a run for it. She grabbed the nearest door handle, Izzie dived inside and Layah pulled the door closed behind them.

# Chapter Six

Layah put her eye to the crack in the door, her pulse racing. Izzie was frozen beside her. The footsteps were in the corridor now, growing louder.

*Tap-tap. Tap-tap.*

For a moment, all Layah could see was a slit of tiles and wall and then – with a hiccup from Layah's stomach – the person came into view. She had been prepared for the yellow eyes and cruel sneer but the figure who emerged was not the woman from the garden – although she was just as strange. She was like a human moth. White skin like torn tissues with wisps of dust-coloured hair. She was bundled up in a coat, leaning on a black cane.

'Is that the woman?' Izzie breathed.

'No . . .' whispered Layah, 'I mean, it's *a* woman but not *the* woman.'

The woman in the corridor was positively ancient. Her eyes were grey and white, like the rest of her, and shone like marbles in the dusty air. For a second Layah thought the woman was going to stop but she carried on down the corridor with her cane – *tap-tap*, *tap-tap* – keys clinking on a chain around her neck. Maybe she was the school caretaker. Layah breathed again as the footsteps faded away.

'Layah . . . I think you should see this.'

Layah turned to see Izzie craning up at a shelf behind the teacher's desk. Layah reached up and took down the object Izzie was straining for. It was a framed photograph, the colours faded by sun and age. A grainy image showed eight girls in white tennis dresses which sagged below their knees; their faces were expressionless smudges. Their teacher, dressed in blotchy black, stood to the side. The date on the frame was some time in the 1980s and under the date were the names: Mistress E. Brown, M. Whitehead, S. Sanderson and . . .

Layah's finger froze on the frame. Her heart stopped.

The next name was jarringly familiar. It was her own. L. Bellford.

'Who . . . who is this?' Layah's voice sounded distant. 'I thought all the Bellfords were gone. I thought Mum said . . .'

Layah gazed at the photograph. At the girl at the end of the row. L. Bellford. Her face was just as blurred and indistinguishable as the others but on her arm she wore a bracelet which looked white in the greyscale photo.

The Bellfords were never spoken about at home. All Layah knew was that her mum's parents had died when she was small and she never spoke about them. Their dad's side, the Kosmatkas, were simply teeming with relatives. Their dad had two older brothers, both of whom had big, boisterous families. Babcia had to cook a vat of *barszcz* soup and a bucket-load of *pierogi* to feed them all at Christmas Eve.

Layah had always wondered about the Bellfords but she had learned not to ask about them – her mum would leave the room and her dad would hang his head and say, 'It's a painful subject.'

Layah darted around the study, peering up at the other photos and sports medals, pulling out drawers and shuffling folders, not bothering about making a mess as she searched for another clue to L. Bellford.

'Layah! What if she comes back?' said Izzie.

'So watch by the door,' fired back Layah, kneeling down to rifle through the waste-paper bin.

A frantic desire was burning inside her. Seeing the name was like seeing familiar eyes in the face of a stranger. Could this person – L. Bellford – be related to her mum? To Layah and Izzie?

At last, Layah had to admit that L. Bellford was nowhere else to be found.

'Izzie, do you know what this means?' said Layah, grabbing the photo again. 'We're not the last Bellfords!'

'It could be a coincidence,' suggested Izzie.

'The same spelling? Two Ls?' Layah drove on. 'What if the woman knows something about the Bellfords and she led me here to find out? And – and that caretaker woman, maybe she let the woman from the garden into the school, that's how she disappeared so quickly when I was chasing her!' Layah's excitement was mounting. 'What if there's some Bellford family secret hidden here – in Lowesdale? Some secret that Mum doesn't want us to know about!'

There was a bang not far off – a door closing. Layah looked around the study, at the ransacked desk and fallen frames.

'We need to go before that caretaker comes back,' whispered Layah, hastily sweeping the papers into a pile.

Izzie slipped the photo of L. Bellford into her rucksack as Layah opened the door.

'Coast seems clear,' said Layah.

Together they crept back the way they had come. The window was – thankfully – still open and Layah helped Izzie up first, before scrambling after her. The two of them started across the courtyard towards the gate.

'Someone's coming!' warned Izzie.

Another door slammed nearby. They didn't have time to climb the railings!

'Get down!' cried Layah.

They dived into the rose bushes, sending the buds quivering, just as the *tap-tap*, *tap-tap* reached their ears. Layah lay still on the ground, breathing soil, her heart hammering. She looked sideways at Izzie, who was white as paper, and gripped her hand reassuringly.

*Tap-tap. Clip-clop.*

There was someone else walking with the caretaker. Layah shifted as gently as she could, craning her neck to see through the thorns. The two people came into view – and Layah had to clasp a hand over her mouth to stop herself gasping.

Their mum was walking beside the caretaker away from the school, her blue raincoat fluttering in the breeze. As they watched, she paused at the gate and the caretaker scrabbled to undo the chain and then, with a last look back at the school, their mum walked away down the street.

Babcia liked to say that 'every family has a story'. What she'd never said was that some have secrets, too.

# Chapter Seven

Layah and Izzie lay flat in the rose bushes as their mum's footsteps faded away. Layah was shaking, her fingers digging into the earth as if worried it might slip away.

'What was Mum doing in the school?' breathed Izzie.

'I doubt she was there for a maths lesson,' mumbled Layah. 'Let's follow her.'

Layah made to spring up, but Izzie clung on to her arm.

'Not yet!' hissed Izzie.

The caretaker was on the other side of the railings, relocking the gate with an iron chain. Layah's foot twitched impatiently, sending a shiver through the rose bush, and the caretaker's head snapped up. Layah and Izzie tensed, petrified, as the caretaker's eyes raked the school yard. Layah held her breath.

*Tap-tap. Tap-tap.*

She looked up to see the caretaker trudging away

towards the high street, in the same direction as their mum.

'Come on!' Layah whispered, the second the caretaker was out of sight.

Layah surged up out of the roses; she gripped the railings and shimmied over. She fell hard on the other side, grazing her knee, but she hobbled up the lane, waving for Izzie to follow.

More secrets! Layah didn't understand. Why would Mum hide the fact that she knew Lowesdale School? That a member of the Bellford family – this L. Bellford – had actually gone there?

Layah reached the high street and paused. The village was packing up for the day; shop fronts were shutting down and a man and his dog scuttled for shelter, sensing the rain in the air. Layah strained this way and that, but there was no sign of their mum or the caretaker. She gave a snort of annoyance.

'Layah, wait!' Izzie was jogging up behind her.

'This proves it!' Layah spun around. 'The connection between the Bellford family and Lowesdale School.'

'Yes, but Mum must have a good reason for keeping the Bellfords a secret,' protested Izzie.

'Stop defending her.' Layah gave her a dark look. 'Iz, this is our family history and we have a right to know about it.'

'But what if it's something horrible?' said Izzie. 'The woman – the one with yellow eyes – she's not normal. You said so yourself. I've got a bad feeling about her! What if she's like a ghost or a bad spirit like in—'

'Stop!' Layah heard herself shout. 'You don't get it, do you? This isn't some magical story. This is real life. Mum is keeping something from us – something about our family – and you're just going to ignore it?'

'That's not—'

Izzie tried to interject but Layah couldn't stop; she felt the words tearing out of her, everything she'd been holding back for months.

'You're so oblivious you haven't even realised that Mum and Dad might be getting a divorce!' Layah stormed. 'You're so obsessed with stories – why can't you just grow up? Mum is lying to us! Dad doesn't care about us – all he cares about is his stupid job! I'm the only one who cares about our family.'

'That's not true! I do care.' Izzie's voice drowned Layah's out. 'I know more than you think. I know what's been going on with Mum and Dad for ages. I know life isn't the same as books because books are better. Books are safe! It doesn't mean I don't care!'

'I didn't mean you don't *care*,' argued Layah, 'I was

just . . . I know it's hard to understand—'

'I do understand! When are you going to realise that?'

Izzie's watery glare stunned Layah into silence. Her anger was draining away and she felt suddenly ashamed.

'Izzie, I'm sorry – I was angry about Mum . . . I didn't mean—'

'I need the bookshop!' Izzie shouted and ran full pelt up the slope.

'Iz! Wait! I'm sorry!'

But Izzie was still running. Layah watched her reach the bookshop and, ignoring the 'closed' sign, she disappeared inside.

Layah was about to trek after her, guilt beating in her chest, when a noise stopped her. The hairs on the back of her neck began to prickle.

It was like the hiss of a kettle, drifting in and out of the wind. Then the whistling began in earnest. Layah looked around her. She could sense the direction the whistling was coming from, but she couldn't see the strange woman. Or anyone else.

With a quick glance at the bookshop – Izzie would be safe in there – Layah began to walk down the hill towards the lake.

She didn't know whether it was stupidity or bravery

but something was urging Layah onwards. She had to prove this wasn't some spooky fantasy.

The Boating Centre was completely deserted and twilight was descending like a soft mist, making her vision fuzzy. Layah dropped down from the road and began to walk along the shingle. She could sense a figure moving somewhere ahead.

Layah crept forward. She was right in between the boats now. The place was eerie, echoing with emptiness. Even the lapping of the lake against the pebbles seemed hushed. The lopsided Wayfarer sailing boats were like giant dead fish.

The crunch of a footstep reached Layah and she realised the whistling had stopped. She had walked even further into the crowd of boats and could barely see the road in the dusk. Another step. Something was just beyond the prow of the nearest boat. Layah suddenly felt foolish and weak. Her arms limp and feeble. What was she doing here? The shuffling continued. She was so close now.

'Hello? Are you the woman who came to our cottage the other night?' Layah fought to keep her voice steady. 'What do you want? Do you know something about our family? About L. Bellford?'

The footsteps had stopped. Layah moved slowly

around the side of the boat. There was nothing there.

'Hello?'

Something powerful grabbed her from behind, pinning her arms to her sides. Her hands grappled, unseeing, with her attacker, latching on to something thick and soft. There were fingers at her throat – Layah twisted vigorously and felt the chain of her amber necklace snap – she was being lifted and dragged backwards, her toes skimming the ground helplessly.

Layah heard someone shouting, 'Hey! Oi!'

She was tossed aside. She fell hard into a Wayfarer and crashed to the ground. There was a thud of new footsteps and suddenly hands were pulling her upright.

'Layah? Layah!'

It was James Westwood, slack-jawed with shock.

'Blimey! Are – are you OK?' he stammered.

Layah's arms and ribs were stinging from the fall. A low buzzing was filling her head as if the volume of the evening had been dialled up. She couldn't remember screaming but her throat was dry.

'I'm fine,' she croaked.

Her body was shaking uncontrollably, and she slumped down again. James looked fearful. He hoisted her up, one arm around her waist. She swayed where she stood, her teeth chattering. James was staring at her hands.

Layah looked down at her clenched fists and gave a gasp of surprise. Uncurling from her sweaty palms were two fistfuls of long, purple-tipped black feathers.

The curtain of ivy was torn aside, the heavy door almost wrenched from its hinges, as the Other forced the girl inside. They were both breathless and mud-flecked. The Other swept through the room, drawing the curtains and dousing the fire.

'Did they see you?' The Other gripped the girl's arms.

'No – no, I don't think—'

'But you can't be sure?'

The girl retreated to her usual hollow by the window, her eyes never leaving the Other. The room was half embedded in the mountainside – the walls running smoothly from brick to rock – pots and pans and bunches of herbs and berries hung over a fireplace.

The Other was mumbling to herself, her agitation filling the air.

'If they saw . . . if our secrets are revealed, it will be dangerous. I was a fool to let you go out in twilight – night is our cover and our protection—'

'They didn't see me,' interrupted the girl, 'I was gone before they could turn.'

'I cannot risk it.'

The Other paused and her face morphed into a smile. The girl's pulse quickened with fear and excitement.

'The food parcels were one thing, but this is different. We will need to act with force,' breathed the Other. 'No more sulking and watching and waiting – now is the moment. We will teach them a lesson – they know too much. They will be punished for their curiosity.'

'But we're safe – I'm safe,' protested the girl. 'What if we just scare them?'

'Mere fear will not keep them at bay this time,' said the Other. 'We are warriors – we are powerful – it is time to use that power. It is time for you to use it.'

'Me?' The girl looked up, cheeks flushed, and her eyes glowed brighter.

'The time is right. It is time for you to step up and show me what you can do.' The Other leered. 'You must exterminate those pests. You must kill them.' The Other rolled the words on her tongue, savouring them.

'Kill? No, I can't . . .'

'No one will suspect,' hissed the Other. 'You are

young. You could slip amongst them without suspicion. Humans' greatest downfall is their trust in others – in foolish things like family and youth. But you can deceive them!' The Other smirked. 'You will use your cunning and your stealth. This is what your lessons have led to. Prove you are not a coward and a weakling.'

'I'm not a weakling,' said the girl quickly.

She stepped up and stood tall – but inside her heart was quivering.

'Then we must act quickly,' said the Other. 'I shall continue to spy on those meddlers and you shall remain here. I want you working on your plan of attack. This must be a show of strength – you must prove you are worthy of the Teachings! You must kill those interfering humans.'

The girl nodded. 'I won't let you down.'

Unseen by the Other, the girl's hand slipped into her pocket and her fist squeezed tight around the object hidden inside.

# CHAPTER EIGHT

The rain had returned by the time James and Izzie carried Layah down the path to Rook Cottage. The bookshop owner had finally persuaded Izzie to leave and James had found her sitting on the shop doorstep. James and Izzie had pushed Layah back on James's Vespa – despite Layah's protests. Above Layah's eye, a bruise was blossoming where she had hit the boat. She could feel it smarting in the cold rain. She couldn't stop shaking.

'Girls! Where on earth have you been?'

Their mum appeared in the doorway, her hair tied up in a bird's-nest bun and her mascara smudged. She gasped when she saw Layah, and dragged her inside and on to the sofa.

'Nasty hit. You're in shock,' Mum muttered. 'We need turmeric. Lemon and ginger tea. Two sugars! Izzie, get the kettle on!'

Izzie and James were standing by the door, both so

wet with rain they looked as if they were melting. Izzie scampered off to the kitchen and James shifted his weight.

'Can I help, Mrs Bellford?'

Layah's mum twitched a smile at him. 'Towels, please! In the cupboard.'

'I'm all right!' moaned Layah.

She heard her mum banging around in her bedroom and the gurgle of the kettle in the kitchen. She wanted to get up but fell back, exhausted. James's face reappeared in front of her, holding a pile of towels. He placed one awkwardly over her shoulders.

'I can't believe something like this would happen in Lowesdale,' said James weakly. 'I mean . . . nothing ever happens here!'

'Glad I could provide some entertainment,' said Layah grimly.

'For a second I thought it might be . . .'

Layah leant forward, wincing slightly. 'You think it was the Lowesdale Stranger. Don't you?'

'No!' James sounded uncertain. 'No, I haven't lost my marbles. The Lowesdale Stranger isn't real, but I suppose . . . maybe there is someone living in the forest? Maybe you ran into him in the dark?'

'You think the Lowesdale Stranger is a man?'

## Hampton Hill Library
68 High Street, Hampton Hill, TW12 1NY

Account: \*\*\*\*\*\*\*4064

The bird singers

Due date: 25/01/23

Total items borrowed: 1

04/01/23 4:00 PM

'I don't know, could be a woman.' James shrugged. 'I mean, I'm not saying I believe it!'

Layah turned this over in her mind. 'You're sure you didn't see anyone in the boatyard?' pressed Layah. 'Like . . . an old woman?'

'No!' James was looking at her as though she'd just asked him whether he'd seen a runaway clown.

Before Layah could respond, her mum came thumping down the stairs, cradling her first-aid bag.

'Excuse me, James. Layah, this will sting but it'll be worth it,' said Mum, sitting cross-legged on the floor in front of her. 'What happened?'

'I'm all right,' Layah said in a gruff wobble.

This didn't seem the best moment to confront her mum about seeing her at the school. Layah didn't fancy admitting how her plans to retrieve information had backfired.

'What happened?' Mum repeated.

'She was attacked, Mrs Bellford,' said James, 'down by the Boating Centre. I scared them off,' he added, with a dashing smile no one saw.

'Layah, what were you doing?' demanded Mum, her face paling.

'Nothing. It's not always my fault, you know.'

Izzie hurried back in, holding the mug of lemon and

ginger tea. Layah took it and sipped, wishing everyone would stop fussing.

'Who was it, James? Did you see?'

'Well . . . um . . . no,' said James uncomfortably. 'I didn't see anyone.'

'Layah! Where's your necklace?' exclaimed Mum.

'Do you mean this?' James pulled the broken chain and amber pendant from his pocket. 'I found it on the ground.'

'I'll fix it,' said Mum, taking it from him.

There was a knock at the door.

'That'll be my father,' groaned James. 'I messaged him what happened.'

Henry Westwood strode into the room with the face of a man who was ready to take charge. He peered down at Layah on the sofa and she noticed a nervousness in his eyes. He placed a strong arm around their mum's shoulders.

'Oh my! Ren! What's happened here?' he drawled.

'Oh, Henry, there was no need for you to come,' said Mum, 'nothing's wrong. We're fine, no need to—'

'Someone attacked Layah,' James told his dad, 'by the Boating Centre.'

'And James stopped them!' pointed out Izzie.

Henry's smile wavered as he eyed his son. 'Good

work, James,' he said, rather brusquely, cuffing his son on the back.

'Yes. Thank you, James,' said Mum, 'thanks for everything. I'm sure it was just a mistake – some confused boater! Henry, there's no need to stay. I've got everything covered.'

'Well, if you're sure, Ren,' said Henry. 'As long as everyone's happy.'

'Wait. Aren't you going to call the police?' said James.

'Oh, James, we don't want to go wasting police time!' scoffed Henry.

'Oh no. It's fine. As long as Layah's all right,' Mum agreed, 'we don't want to make a fuss.'

Layah and Izzie exchanged confused looks as their mum chivvied Henry and James out of the room.

The front door slammed.

'You need a hot bath,' said Mum, business-like. 'You're covered in dirt. So are you, Iz! Looks like you've both been sitting in a plant pot! Right. Iz, make another cup of tea. I'll get the bath ready.'

'I'm OK,' insisted Layah, unwilling to admit that her legs felt like rubber.

'Yes, yes. Just lie there while we get everything ready,' soothed her mum.

Layah rolled her eyes but sank thankfully into the

cushions as they hurried away.

From the sofa, Layah noticed that one of the windows was open, rain spotting the carpet. Through the gap she could hear Henry and James's voices, low but distinct. Layah craned her neck to listen.

'I don't know what you were thinking of,' Henry was saying, fumbling with his car keys. 'Why were you hanging around by the lake?'

'I didn't do anything wrong!'

'For goodness' sake, James! I don't want you getting mixed up in this.'

'Mixed up in what?' James spluttered.

'I can't handle a scandal!' snapped Henry. 'If the local newspapers heard you were involved in this. . . The new hotel deal hasn't gone through yet and I can't afford any bad press.'

'*I* didn't attack her!' cried James. 'I just wanted to help.'

'James! Get on that damned scooter. We'll continue this later. I've had just about enough of you!'

A car door banged. The silver Jaguar revved angrily then shot off, the headlights bouncing over the hedgerows, followed by the whine of James's Vespa. Layah lay back on the sofa. For the first time, she reflected on how it must feel to have Henry as a father.

Her dad might be pathetic and spineless, but at least he wasn't Henry. She felt a stab of sympathy for James. She shouldn't have been so spiky with him. It was just possible she'd misjudged him. Layah touched the bruise on her face. She felt the shock wearing off and questions replacing it, thudding like a headache.

# CHAPTER NINE

That night, dark shapes invaded Layah's dreams, needling her with fear. She dreamed she was running through the boatyard, slipping on a carpet of photographs and feathers, following someone ahead of her. The figure looked back and there was a flash of yellow eyes – then a piercing light broke into her sleep and Layah woke, muddled and sweating. She could still see the beam of light and, blinking, she realised it was coming from outside her curtained window.

Without waking Izzie, she crept across the room and peered out. It was a torch. As it swept through the garden, she recognised the outline of her mum. She was moving slowly around Rook Cottage, shining the torch this way and that in the darkness. *What is she doing?* Layah thought. The torch suddenly swung towards Layah's window and she ducked, her heart beating wildly. Then the beam disappeared around a corner of the cottage. Layah stole back to bed and lay still, her mind racing.

Layah woke up the next morning with her neck aching and her limbs feeling cramped and out of place. She couldn't remember why she was so uncomfortable. But then – slowly and painfully – the memories of the attack resurfaced, and with them, a surge of adrenaline.

A frying pan crackled in the kitchen below and Layah's stomach rumbled. Maybe she had been too harsh on her mum. If she really was trying to hide a Bellford family secret, she must have her reasons. Maybe her mum was downstairs now, waiting to explain everything.

Layah slipped out of bed and headed downstairs. As she passed through the living room she saw a folded blanket and a torch on the sofa. She remembered seeing a similar bundle of sheets – which she'd taken for dirty laundry – the morning after she'd seen the strange woman in the garden. Had their mum started sleeping down here?

Layah entered the kitchen and was surprised to find Izzie alone, one hand on the frying pan and a book in the other. A sandwich box containing the feathers that Layah had torn from her attacker sat on the kitchen table. Their purple-black plumage glinted in the morning sunlight. Beside it, the framed photo of the tennis team with L. Bellford, and – Layah couldn't help smiling – her necklace, the broken chain patched up with a ribbon from one of her mum's dresses. The air was smoky but when Layah tried to open a window she found it jammed. A thick glue had been applied to the window panes, sealing them shut.

'What's next?' tutted Layah. 'Is she going to barricade the front door so we can't get out? If she's so worried about security, why doesn't she just tell us the truth! Where is she anyway?'

'She left a note.' Izzie pointed to the table.

Layah picked up the orange Post-it and read:

Layah and Iz –

I'm out for a walk. Back this afternoon. Layah, you need rest!

Love Mum xx

PS. Henry dropped off bikes this morning. Wait until I'm back before you go out! X

'Bet she's gone for breakfast at Westwood Manor.' Layah slumped into a chair.

Their mum couldn't be bothered to wait and see how

Layah was feeling. Her sympathy for her daughter stretched to the size of a Post-it note!

At home, Mum would always be there, the morning after an argument, ready to make up over toast and Nutella. She'd always put Layah and Izzie first. It was Dad who was forever making excuses – 'I know it's your art show, Layah, but I've been invited to a lecture on insomnia in nocturnal mammals . . .' In the end, Layah stopped inviting him to things. Now she had two parents who didn't care.

'Her walking boots are gone,' observed Izzie, closing her book.

'Maybe she and Henry have gone for a walk together – I bet she wouldn't mind him tagging along. Or she's sneaking off to the school again,' said Layah, fiddling with the box of feathers. 'You didn't tell mum about the photograph, did you?'

'It didn't come up.'

'These feathers are weird, aren't they?' said Layah. 'The attacker must have been wearing a funny kind of coat.'

'Do you want sausage and scrambled egg on toast?' interrupted Izzie. 'It's the last of the *kiełbasa* sausage from home.'

'Oh, yes please!'

Izzie handed over a plate and Layah crunched gratefully into the toast. The sausage had a smoky, peppery taste, a flavour of family mornings in Babcia's steamy kitchen. Both sisters sat and munched for a few minutes.

'Mum misses Dad,' said Izzie quietly.

Layah gave a disbelieving snort.

'I heard her listening to Polish Radio this morning,' continued Izzie, trailing her eggs around her plate. 'You know she doesn't understand it and she hates the music . . . I miss him too.'

'Yeah, well . . . his work is more important,' mumbled Layah. 'He'll forget my birthday without Mum to remind him.'

They continued to eat in silence.

'Hey, Izzie.' Layah took a deep breath. 'I'm sorry about yesterday . . . about saying you didn't care about Mum and Dad and everything. I know I've been a massive grump lately. And I'm sorry.'

'It's OK,' said Izzie, 'I'm sorry too but . . . did you really think I had no idea what was going on? I do read a lot of mystery books, you know.'

Layah laughed. 'So why didn't you say anything to me at home?'

'I didn't want to upset you,' said Izzie meekly.

'I didn't want to upset *you*!' Layah laughed again.

It suddenly all seemed so comical – why hadn't she just talked to Izzie about everything from the beginning? Layah grinned at her sister.

'Thanks, Iz, for coming with me to the school. For being on my side.'

'So what shall we do about L. Bellford?' said Izzie, pulling the frame towards them. 'I think maybe you're right – maybe we do deserve to know the truth. Maybe it'll help us understand who the strange woman you've been seeing everywhere is, and if it's all connected.'

'I agree,' said Layah. 'But I just don't know where to start. What would they do in your mystery books?'

'I've had an idea actually.' Izzie beamed. 'We should return to the scene of the crime – the Boating Centre – and look for clues.'

'Let's do it!'

Layah felt a sudden lightness in her chest. Even if their mum had turned her back on her, Layah wasn't alone. It wasn't just the sausage and scrambled eggs. There was no doubt about it, Layah had found her ally.

Layah had expected Henry's bicycles to be sparkly pink and have unicorn handlebars but the girls were in luck. They were sturdy mountain bikes with a decent grip on the slippery roads. The wind had not abated and the trees above them thrashed as the sisters cycled down to Lowesdale. It had taken both their combined strength to pry open the cottage door, as the wind kept slamming it shut.

Cycling always reminded Layah of her dad and the summer he'd taught her to ride. He'd driven her out to the park, just the two of them. Layah recalled howling with laughter when her dad, attempting to demonstrate an emergency stop, had tumbled headfirst into the pond. Now, Layah's bike was rusting in their garden shed. It was too dangerous to cycle on the roads in London and her dad didn't have time to drive her to the park any more. His work had to come first. As always.

It was another dull day in Lowesdale. The residents were making the most of the break in the rain. The Boating Centre was, as usual, empty of customers. Gulls gathered on the upturned boats, their pointed faces turned towards a lifeguard as he stacked canoes. The lake was deep blue today, spreading smoothly across to the distant shore. Above it all, the mottled slopes of the Lowesdale Giant yawned up to meet a grey-white sky. The shadows of clouds skittered across the mountainside.

Layah followed Izzie down amongst the boats. It felt strange to be there in daylight; all the eeriness of the place seemed to have evaporated.

'OK!' Izzie surveyed the area. 'Now I'll check around here – the location of the attack – and you can walk that way and see if the attacker left anything when they ran away.'

'Right. Let me know if you find anything.'

Layah left Izzie kneeling between two boats and walked slowly back the way they had come, shifting the shingle with her shoes. She wasn't overly hopeful that they would find anything, but it was better than doing nothing. Her thoughts turned to her mum. What had she been doing in the garden last night? Was she looking for something? Or someone? The old woman, perhaps. If her mum knew who the woman was, was it possible they had arranged some kind of midnight meeting?

'Hunting for monsters, are you?'

Layah jumped and looked up to see James Westwood leaning against a nearby Wayfarer.

'Morning.' He said. 'What you doing? Searching for clues?'

'No,' said Layah defensively. James raised an eyebrow. 'Fine. Yes, but it was Izzie's idea.'

James looked a lot sunnier than he had last night: his confident swagger was back.

'The myth-busting Londoner captures the Lowesdale Stranger!' He grinned. 'Well, if you need any help solving the mystery, let me know.'

'It can't be a mystery that I find you incredibly annoying!' said Layah, rolling her eyes.

'Oh, that one I solved.' He smirked. 'The Case of the Butting-in Boy!'

Layah laughed, despite herself. James looked pleased.

'Jokes aside, I've got something to show you.'

He unfolded a crumpled sheet of paper and held it out to her. It was covered in an untidy scrawl:

### Help Friend On Lake Now

'Someone chucked it at me last night,' explained James. 'I was just doodling along on the Vespa and then this hits my visor – almost cracked the glass! It was wrapped in a button.'

'A button?'

'You wouldn't happen to know anything about this? Did your sister write it?'

'This definitely isn't Izzie's handwriting,' said Layah, turning the message over in her hands. 'And why would she throw this at you? Why wouldn't she just talk to you?'

Layah read the message again. She wasn't sure whether James was playing some sort of prank on her. But if he was telling the truth then it meant someone had watched her go down to the lake. Someone knew she needed help. Did she have a secret friend in Lowesdale?

'Do you really think it was the Lowesdale Stranger who attacked me last night?' said Layah.

James took a step back.

'Woah! That's not what I said,' he protested, 'I don't believe that rubbish! I said it could be someone the villagers *think* is the Lowesdale Stranger. Some ordinary person who inspired the stories.'

'All myths are based on truth,' muttered Layah, thinking of Babcia.

'Exactly!' James nodded.

'But what do the stories say?' asked Layah, handing back the note.

'The myth of the Lowesdale Stranger has been going on for decades.' James's voice dropped to a dramatic whisper. 'There were always stories about people getting lost on the Lowesdale Giant or getting killed in freak snowstorms – sheep and cows going missing, prize pumpkins pulled up by the roots. But one midnight, a lady saw a figure in the churchyard, feasting on dead rabbits, and she chased the creature up the mountain until it vanished into the trees. From then on, the villagers knew they were cursed by a shadow: the Lowesdale Stranger, stalking the countryside at night!' James paused for breath and grinned.

'So it's a creature? Do you mean an animal?' prompted Layah.

'I always thought they meant it was like a werewolf,' said James. 'But I have a theory – I think the Lowesdale Stranger is actually an old hippy living in the woods and stealing food from the village. The kind of guy who weaves grass pants and talks to trees. And last night proves that the Stranger is a coward – I scared it off just by shouting at it! A monster wouldn't have run off like that. But the Stranger didn't want us to see his face.'

Layah considered this theory. She wondered whether she should share her information about the strange woman in the garden, but something told her to go cautiously where James Westwood was concerned.

'And you want to unmask the Lowesdale Stranger,' said Layah, 'and prove it's a fake?'

'Yes!' James beamed enthusiastically. 'Think of the scandal!'

Layah was about to ask more but her gaze was caught by a commotion at the end of the road. A cloud of seagulls was squawking and jostling around a hunched figure. Layah recognised the wizened caretaker from the school, her grey eyes glaring in the sunlight as she threw breadcrumbs for the birds.

'James, who's that woman?' said Layah. 'She's from the school, right?'

James gave her a curious look; Layah didn't know whether he was going to laugh at her.

'You're really getting into this Lowesdale folklore stuff, aren't you?' He grinned. 'That's Mor Hemlock, the school caretaker. I'd keep away from her if I were you. I heard she's really awful to the students. Apparently, she locked a girl in a shed once for dropping a crisp packet in the playground – and she chopped off one girl's ponytail just for climbing a tree!'

'And has she got anything to do with the Lowesdale Stranger?'

James's smirk widened. 'Funny you should ask,' he said, his eyes dancing. 'Many say it was Mor Hemlock who first saw the Lowesdale Stranger in the churchyard, and that she's been working for the Stranger ever since

– stealing injured sheep and drowned rats to give to her master on the mountain. Whatever she is – she's creepy.'

Layah watched Mor Hemlock from behind the boat. She might look wispy but there was a toughness about her, like a woodlouse with a bad temper. No sooner had Layah thought it, Mor Hemlock jabbed her cane at a passing dog, who'd tried to take a snap at the birds, and it yelped pitifully.

'If you want to find out more about Mor Hemlock, maybe we could tail her?' said James. 'We could dress up like two birds and flap around her – I'm sure she won't notice – we could use the wetsuits, stick on some feathers and—'

'Izzie and I have plans.' Layah gave him a be-serious look. 'And – I dunno – it could be dangerous.'

She regretted saying this at once. James was looking at her with a mixture of disappointment and disbelief.

'Layah, none of these stories are real!' He gawped.

'It felt pretty real last night!' retorted Layah, flushing pink. 'When I was having my neck twisted in the dark.'

'What were you even doing creeping around the boats?' asked James. 'You're lucky I was there to save you.'

'I don't need saving!'

James's smile dropped. 'Fine! Fair enough. I've got better things to do anyway.'

He tried to sound causal, but Layah caught the bitterness in his tone. He turned on his heel and marched back towards his Vespa in the road. 'And you're wasting your time,' he called back, 'I didn't see any footprints. The attacker just disappeared into thin air.'

And with that, he swung his leg on to his Vespa and rode away.

'Well, that sounded friendly,' said Izzie, popping up from behind a boat. 'Shall we go for a scone?'

Layah growled. She couldn't work out what James wanted. Did he actually want to help them or was he just messing them around?

At the end of the road, Mor Hemlock threw the last of her crumbs and the gulls dived for them. She tottered around and started tap-tapping away up the high street. Layah watched a blackbird glide over the gulls and follow the caretaker up the street. The sight made her feel uneasy.

# Chapter Ten

The fresh rain and Izzie's request for 'proper scones' drove the sisters inside the Old Singer Tea Room. They huddled against the rain-splatted window; the steamed-up glass made it look like the whole village was underwater. The tea room was an old-fashioned place. The walls were a patchwork of china plates and customers balanced on antique furniture. The menu was not as exciting as the Boat Café – crumbling shortbread and flat lemon cake could never compete with toffee apple crumble – but where the tea room did triumph was its scones; fluffy and still warm from the oven, they had the perfect raisin-to-dough ratio.

Izzie was engrossed in loading her scone with butter, jam and clotted cream but Layah wasn't hungry. They had placed the framed photograph of the tennis team next to the teapot and Layah couldn't stop staring at L. Bellford's blurred face. She couldn't explain it, but she felt such a strong connection to the girl in the photograph. It felt like she was gazing into a foggy mirror. Layah knew Babcia wouldn't approve of their sneaking around, but Babcia had been a firm believer in understanding the past. They were simply trying to unravel their own family secret.

'If we're going to proceed with this investigation,' said Izzie, patiently adding more clotted cream to her scone mountain, 'we need to lay down the facts. That usually helps.'

'OK. At last count, we've got two dead birds, two strange women – Mor Hemlock and the woman in the garden – let's call her the Midnight Visitor,' said Layah, 'and one photograph. It's not much to go on.'

'It just needs a bit of thought,' said Izzie, raising her scone theatrically, 'and we shall get to the bottom of this mystery together!'

Layah flicked tea in Izzie's direction.

'Be serious, Iz.' Then she was suddenly struck by an idea. 'Hey, hang on! What if the birds weren't even meant for us? What if they're nothing to do with the L. Bellford mystery? What about Henry?' said Layah. 'I mean, they were thrown at his cottage and on the road he's always driving down. And he's got this hotel deal coming up – maybe it was a message from a business rival.'

Izzie considered this idea, licking crumbs from her fingers.

'Forget the birds for a moment,' continued Layah. 'I reckon someone attacked me because they knew we'd found the photo of L. Bellford and they're trying to scare us off.'

'The attacker broke Babcia's necklace,' said Izzie thoughtfully.

'Well, it kind of broke in the struggle. I don't know if they were actually aiming for it.'

'Is Polish amber expensive?' pondered Izzie. 'Maybe the attacker wanted to steal it?'

Layah shrugged. 'Yeah, maybe.'

'And you said James thought it was the Lowesdale Stranger,' said Izzie. 'Is the Lowesdale Stranger the Midnight Visitor – or someone else?'

'James reckons this Lowesdale Stranger is a hippy who lives on the mountain, but I think it must be the Midnight Visitor. It's got to be! James said the villagers think the Lowesdale Stranger is some kind of creature but . . . that's obviously ridiculous.'

Layah searched her sister's face, hoping for agreement, but Izzie didn't look up. She was gazing into her teacup, frowning slightly.

'I know there's a difference between books and real

life,' Izzie said carefully. 'I'm not saying unicorns exist. I just think the villagers might be right and the Midnight Visitor – the Lowesdale Stranger – is unnatural . . . she's dangerous.'

'Yeah, but a creature? A monster?' scoffed Layah, finally tucking into her scone.

'Layah, you said she had yellow eyes!'

'I could have imagined it,' protested Layah valiantly. 'It could have been a mask or make-up, or something. Let's not get carried away.'

Sensing Layah's unease, Izzie tactfully changed the subject. 'So where does L. Bellford come into it?' she asked.

'If anyone doesn't want us finding out about the Bellfords, it's Mum,' said Layah. 'Remember how determined she was for us not to call the police? Maybe Mum—'

'No.' Izzie lowered her teacup. 'Layah, no. Mum would never want anyone to hurt us.'

'Then what was she doing sneaking around the garden last night?' challenged Layah. 'She knows something about the Midnight Visitor. I can just feel it.'

'Mum would never hurt us,' repeated Izzie sternly.

Layah gritted her teeth, but Izzie was right. No matter how angry and frustrated Layah was with her mum, she knew she would never ever harm them. She'd do anything to keep them safe – just as Layah would do anything for Mum and Izzie.

'Fine.' Layah slumped back in her chair, staring at the photograph.

'Have you considered that L. Bellford in the photo might be Mum?' suggested Izzie.

'Mum went to school in London. That's where she met Dad and Henry.'

Babcia had lived in London for ten years when their dad was a teenager. She'd been offered a position at a London university – the only woman in the ancient history department. By the time Babcia was ready to return to Poland, their dad had met their mum and decided to stay.

'Freshen your teapot, dears?'

The woman who ran the tea rooms was standing by their table. She wore a Victorian maid's outfit, which – like everything else in Lowesdale – looked a little worse for wear; the frilly apron was blotchy with butter.

'Yes, please.' Izzie smiled.

The tea lady nudged the photograph as she poured the hot water.

'That from the school, is it?' She nodded.

'Um . . . yes,' said Layah, 'do you know it?'

'Went there myself, dear. I knew Mistress Brown and all.'

'Mistress . . .?'

The tea lady indicated the teacher standing to the side of the group. *Mistress E. Brown,* said the caption below.

'Does she still live round here?' asked Izzie.

'Oh no,' said the tea lady, scratching her chin with the sugar spoon, 'she's moved up to Newbeck. Got a lovely cottage – Wickerberry Cottage, on Primrose Street.'

'And do you know this student? L. Bellford?' said Layah quickly.

The tea lady's brow creased at the name and she flicked her head as if shaking off a fly. 'No,' she said firmly, 'no, I don't.'

She bustled away. Layah wondered if the tea lady had been irritated by the question, or maybe she just didn't like people being nosy.

Izzie grinned across the table. 'Our next line of enquiry is clear,' she whispered. 'We go to Newbeck and track down Mistress Brown and find out what she knows about L. Bellford. The mystery continues!'

# Chapter Eleven

Two and a half scones and two biscuits later, the rain had given up and Layah and Izzie went to inspect the bus timetable. The bus to Newbeck ran once every two hours – there was no way they'd be able to get there and back before evening. The skyline was pinkish purple; twilight was already looming on the horizon. So the two sisters turned their bikes in the direction of Rook Cottage.

Mum had messaged Layah earlier:

**Where are you, girls? Layah, I told you to rest! I'm back for dinner – make sure you're back before dark! Will make macaroni cheese – promise not to burn it this time. XX**

Layah had no idea how her mum knew they were out, especially if she was still out herself. Probably with Henry, Layah reminded herself and felt a wave of irritation.

As they rounded a steep bend, Layah's attention was

caught by a person up ahead. For a second, she was sure it was the Midnight Visitor and her bike swerved – causing Izzie to yell in surprise – but it was a stranger.

The figure was bending over a small something in the road and, with a shudder, Layah realised it was the first dead bird. The man knelt beside it, tools flashing in his hands.

'Hey! What are you doing?' Layah called, surprised by her own daring.

The man hopped up from the ground and cowered. Layah stared. He was the most peculiar person they had yet seen. Clad in autumnal tweed, he wore an old-fashioned cape which drooped like wings over his angular frame and a red bow tie was pinned at his throat.

Layah came to a stop, legs astride her bike. 'What were you doing with that bird?' she demanded.

The man's eyes darted between them, as if considering flight. It was Izzie, dismounting from her bike, who stepped forward, holding out her hand as if he was a wild animal.

'Were you trying to help it?' said Izzie kindly. 'I think it's been dead a few days now.'

'She was a tree sparrow,' chirped the man, 'a pretty little thing. Her death is part of a much bigger hunt which is sweeping our county. She was not

95

the predator's intended target.'

Layah eyed this man warily. He seemed as strange as Mor Hemlock.

'But what of you, little person?' He squinted at Izzie. 'On a school trip, are we? Off to enjoy the countryside?'

'Do you know about birds?' asked Izzie.

'Iz, let's get going, Mum'll be back soon,' called Layah, still on her bike.

The man scuttled towards Izzie and whipped out a card from beneath his cape.

'Teddington Speckleback, at your service,' he twittered. 'How may I assist you on this riotous school excursion? For geography, is it?'

'We're not on a school trip! Izzie, come on!' said Layah, trying to hide her desperation.

Izzie took the calling card and gave Mr Speckleback a polite smile before skipping over to Layah.

'Layah, he's a twitcher – a birdwatcher!' she whispered. 'Maybe he can help identify the feathers.'

'Feathers? Those feathers aren't from a bird. The attacker didn't have a bird under their arm – *Izzie*!'

Layah had a strange feeling about Mr Speckleback: she didn't trust him. It was growing cold, and the afternoon light was fading fast. But Izzie was already unzipping her rucksack and tugging out the box of purple-black feathers.

'What's this? Packed lunch?' said Mr Speckleback, ignoring Layah.

'Feathers,' said Izzie carefully. 'Could you have a look at them and tell us what you think?'

'Ah!' His eyes shone as he took the box and snapped the catch. 'Very nice. Beautiful colour. Black glossed purple – *Pica pica* – must be a member of the crow family . . . carnivorous no doubt and yet . . .'

'Are they real feathers?' asked Izzie.

'Real? Oh yes. You can see it from the stems. The bone there.'

Izzie leant in to see and Layah, finally dismounting her bike, watched with narrowed eyes. Mr Speckleback was twirling a feather in his hands, twittering excitedly to himself.

'Well, now, the closest I can diagnose is *Corvus corax*, all-black, glossy. Raven,' he said thoughtfully. 'And yet it's not quite right. This purple is most unusual . . .'

He peered up at Izzie's encouraging smile.

'This feather is different to any feather I have ever seen . . . So . . . it's not a fake. It's not a mistake. It must be a new species. I knew this was going to be a good Thursday!'

'But how can it be a new species?' said Layah, frowning.

'I know my feathers,' breathed Mr Speckleback, 'from albatross to zebra-waxbill; believe me, I know my birds. And I tell you, missy, this is no species which has yet been documented.' He looked keenly at Izzie. 'Where did you get it? Where is the bird?'

'Technically,' Layah started, 'we don't know where—'

'A woman,' said Izzie, cutting Layah off.

There was a beat and Mr Speckleback ruffled his cape, shifting his gaze between them.

'This is a very strange school trip,' he said at last, 'and you are very strange young ladies.'

'We're not on a school trip!' interjected Layah; a chill was creeping up her spine.

'Do you believe us?' said Izzie softly.

Mr Speckleback said nothing for a moment, humming and tapping his fingers together.

'People believe lots of things,' he said, nodding. 'I could believe you are lying yet that would lead me to lie to myself.'

'What do you mean?' said Layah impatiently.

He looked at her. Something in his flapping manner seemed to have hardened. The eccentric character had vanished and a wily, cunning man took his place. Despite his ancient appearance, he looked strong and wiry, capable of grabbing someone in the dark. Mr

Speckleback tilted his head and gazed with mechanical stillness into Layah's face.

'There are myths of women who grow feathers,' he whispered, 'stories which some have chosen to forget. Stories from ancient times. Deadly tales of shapeshifting fiends – creatures that are half-woman and half-bird – with cruel hearts and terrible powers. The tales say they once helped humans in battle, and took hideous revenge on those who scorned them.'

There was a cold breeze in the air; the leaves of the hedgerow seemed to shiver. It made the hairs on Layah's neck prickle uncomfortably.

'And you think these feathers could have come from one of those women, Mr Speckleback?' probed Izzie.

'Anything is possible.' He nodded. 'I have been waiting for such a discovery. I have felt something in the air of late; the birds of Lowesdale are agitated.'

'Do you think someone in the village could have been helping them? Mor Hemlock, perhaps?' asked Izzie curiously.

'I never speak ill of my fellows!' But Mr Speckleback looked fearful. 'There is great danger afoot. I can tell you tales. I have books of—'

'C'mon, really?' Layah had found her voice. '*Really*? We're not dealing with some bird-woman here. Iz?

Don't let him scare you.'

'Layah, let's just listen to what he has to say,' pleaded Izzie.

'And get pulled into this ridiculous, made-up charade?' said Layah. 'Come on, Izzie. He just wants money or something. I'm sorry. We need to go back.'

'No money!' Mr Speckleback squeaked, dropping back into his twittering performance. 'I'm not selling. I am simply pursuing the truth.' He looked directly at Izzie. 'I have an establishment, in the village. If you ever need me, I shall be waiting. But now, your sister is right, you must go. If what you say is true, there is something evil roaming Lowesdale. Darkness rumbles; I fear the creature will be bolder at night. You have my card. Now go.'

He was already scuttling off back towards the village, the dead tree sparrow limp in his hand.

Layah waited for Izzie to set off then kicked her bike after her, up the deserted road. The sun was almost set now; a few streaks of purple and gold slit the sky open.

Layah breathed deeply, trying to force herself to remain calm.

'People have been imagining monsters for hundreds of years,' Babcia had said once, when Layah's mum complained that her stories were giving Layah nightmares. 'The stories are designed to scare, because they must *teach* and *warn*.' But that didn't mean the monsters were real. These village myths were exactly that – entertainment for gullible tourists, cautionary tales to stop kids staying out late. Layah couldn't allow herself to be fooled! Izzie might believe them but that just meant Layah had to keep a clear head. She couldn't let the weird Mr Speckleback frighten them.

Only there was something he'd said . . . a phrase he'd used which had been oddly familiar . . .

Layah changed the gears as she strained up the hill. They were on the final stretch before the cottage. The trees were thicker here and leant heavily over the road, black shadows pooling from their roots.

A sudden squawk at ground level made Layah clamp on her brakes. She screamed and zigzagged. The bike sprung away from her and she hit the road with a painful thwack; her bike keeled over into the ditch.

'Layah! Are you OK?' Izzie was beside her, pulling her up.

Layah looked around in confusion just in time to see a giant crow launching into the sky, leaving behind all that remained of its field mouse dinner.

One of Layah's knees was bleeding; her leggings were ripped.

'Oh great!' she sighed. 'First my face and now—'

They both turned at once. They'd heard a noise from behind them, beyond the bend in the road.

'Is someone following us?' asked Izzie.

'No,' said Layah, 'I don't think—'

It was unmistakable: the slap and scrape of footsteps. Someone was walking up the hill.

'Do you think it's Mr Speckleback?' whispered Izzie.

It didn't sound like the light-footed birdwatcher. Someone else was stalking towards them, the thickness of the trees hiding their approach.

'Get on your bike,' insisted Layah. 'Go!'

'Layah, I can't leave you—'

'I'm fine!'

Panic was welling up inside her. Layah limped over to her bike and picked it up. The chain had become dislodged. She didn't have time to fix it. 'Izzie. Get going!'

The footsteps were coming closer and faster.

'No. I'm not leaving you.' Izzie's small face turned towards the thicket; Layah could see her knuckles white on her handlebars.

Layah looked wildly around for something to protect them with. The footsteps were almost upon them, and whoever they belonged to was about to turn the bend.

*The hideout on the mountain had a bedroom. More cavern than room. Rocky walls, sloping ceiling and a hollow for the bed. A desk made from a tree trunk and a wooden plank.*

*Rain dashed against the porthole window. The sound agitated the glass. The girl looked up at the rain, then down to her desk, a slight frown on her forehead.*

*The girl was plotting her attack and the desk was a flurry of papers.*

*She picked up the list the Other had given her. Information on her three targets: eye colour, hair colour, height, weight, age, bodily weaknesses. The girl picked up her pencil and began to draw.*

*She sketched them standing together – like a family portrait – imagining their faces. She had only ever glimpsed the three humans she had been ordered to kill.*

*She began to draw other things: a sunny smile, laughter sharing a family joke, a hand on the shoulder . . .*

*No! She would not let emotions weaken her!*

The girl snatched up her drawing and tore it in two, then four, then again and again, until it was scattered across the floor. She backed away from the desk, breathing hard. She clamped her eyes shut and the window banged open. The rain peppered her face and a gust of wind surged into the room, lifting her hair and upsetting the items on the desk.

The girl opened her eyes – glistening and toxic yellow – and she stood amidst a swirl of papers and pens as they spiralled around and around the room.

'Enough!' the girl cried.

She dropped to her knees and the wind fell with her. The window creaked on its hinges. The rain played gently across the desk. The papers floated softly to the floor and lay there like fallen snow.

The girl reached out and picked up something from the mess. It was a note which read:

## For the Stranger on the mountain

She had salvaged this note from one of the food parcels in the forest.

More had arrived since the first. Full of packets of biscuits and cylindrical objects with odd labels like 'baked beans' *and* 'tomato soup'. *The Other had destroyed them. All except one, which the girl had found on her own. The biscuits had been like nothing she'd ever tasted – crumbling and rich – almost as good as that other sweet thing. Chocolate.*

*She wondered if the family of three – her targets – liked chocolate and biscuits.*

*'This is wrong,' she whispered. 'I can't kill them.' And she lay back on the floor, her face wet. 'I won't.'*

*The girl sat up. Her mind had cleared. She pulled a bag from under the bed and silently began to fill it. Paper, her colouring pens, pencils, apples, nuts and blankets. She glanced at the bedroom door; there was silence. It was now or never. She hoisted up her bag on to her shoulders and slipped out of the window.*

# Chapter Twelve

Layah's fists were clenched on her handlebars as she turned to face the approaching footsteps, her blood pumping. Could she use the bike as a weapon? Izzie stood beside her, her face colourless and panicked.

Suddenly, the figure emerged, revealing the sloping walk and bespectacled face of—

'Dad!' Izzie shouted.

Izzie flung her bike to the ground and ran down the hill. She threw her arms around Seb Kosmatka. Their dad looked utterly relieved as he squeezed Izzie back. He looked up at Layah, tweaking his glasses, smiling with his familiar apologetic smile.

'Dad?' Layah felt dull with shock. 'What are you doing here?'

Her words felt thick, like something was constricting her throat. The second she'd seen him she'd wanted to jump into his arms like a little kid. Then a storm cloud had crossed her heart, a fog of broken promises.

'I'm here now,' Dad called to her. 'I'm here and it's all OK.'

Layah folded her arms, her chest squeezing painfully. 'OK' wasn't going to fix anything.

He looked out of place, as if he had been cut out and pasted on the wrong background. He was carrying his tatty rucksack, wearing his faded *Geek Out!* T-shirt under his denim jacket. He had dark lines below his eyes and a rough stubbly beard. He looked as sleep-deprived as their mum.

'Layah, sweetheart,' he croaked, half-raising the arm which wasn't around Izzie. 'What's happened to your face?'

'Fell over,' said Layah curtly.

Izzie was staring at Layah expectantly, waiting for Layah to share in her excitement.

'Does Mum know you're here?' said Layah.

'No, I thought I'd make it a surprise,' said Dad, Izzie beaming beside him.

'This is brilliant! I can't believe you've come!' Izzie grinned. 'Dad, we need to take you to the Boat Café and the Singer Tea Room – their scones are amazing!'

'I always trust the Bellford sisters' judgement when it comes to scones!' He grinned sheepishly. 'We can go for breakfast tomorrow!'

'So they didn't need you at work, huh?' said Layah waspishly.

She turned and started pushing her bike up the hill, the corners of her eyes prickling.

'Layah! Slow down,' Dad called wearily. 'I'm sorry I didn't come sooner, I just thought – since your mum needed some space – and the conference in Denmark . . . but I've taken the next two weeks off! And I'm here for your birthday tomorrow.'

'My birthday's not until next week, Dad,' murmured Layah.

She walked faster. The track to Rook Cottage came into view and beyond it their mum walking down the hill towards them. She looked up, a smile wilting from her face as she saw their dad.

'Hi, Ren,' said Dad, giving a lopsided wave.

Their mum's cheeks flushed scarlet. Whatever joyful reunion their dad had been hoping for was not going to happen.

'Where have you been?' Mum said, looking accusingly at Layah and Izzie. 'I told you to stay in the cottage. Did you know your dad was coming?'

'No, Mum,' sighed Layah.

She caught Izzie's eye and both sisters scurried indoors, sensing an argument brewing. They left their dad behind; he was starting to look like a puppy who had eaten his mistress's favourite shoes. Layah glanced back at him – her throat was still tight but a small part of her was glad he'd come.

The next morning, Layah and Izzie's plans to visit Newbeck were put on hold. At breakfast, their mum announced that she'd arranged another boating trip with Henry – and she reluctantly agreed that their dad could tag along. She had also slipped it into conversation that perhaps their dad should take Layah and Izzie home soon – which Layah found highly suspicious. Why did Mum want to bundle them off back to London? Layah only hoped they would have enough time to visit Mistress Brown and ask her about L. Bellford.

The sisters had spent most of the evening stuck in their bedroom, trying to ignore their parents' arguments, rising like hot steam from the kitchen below. The only good thing about having their dad around was decent cooking. After the arguing had stopped, he made a spread of potato *placki*, stuffed cabbage parcels and fried mushrooms.

Layah was intrigued to visit Westwood Manor – she'd been imagining James living in a palace with butlers and maidservants. The real Westwood Manor, although smaller than a palace, was just as imposing. A wide, sandy driveway ended in fat stone pillars, guarding the front door. The white walls and high windows made Layah think of horse-drawn carriages and ladies in hooped skirts.

Layah and Izzie lagged behind their parents as they approached the house.

'Layah, I know you don't want to consider that the Midnight Visitor is . . . well . . . different,' said Izzie slowly, 'but there was something Mr Speckleback mentioned which reminded me of a poem Babcia translated. It was when he said—'

'"Shapeshifting fiends".' Layah nodded. 'I knew I'd heard it before. The poem about a king who enslaves a monster or something like that. I can't remember. What was it called?'

'"King Vukasin and Mandalina",' supplied Izzie automatically.

'It's probably just a coincidence,' said Layah hopefully.

'I don't know,' whispered Izzie, 'I think Mr Speckleback was trying to warn us.'

'Hurry up, slowpokes!' called Mum, and Izzie pattered off to catch up with their parents.

A movement in an upstairs window caught Layah's attention. James was looking down at them. Layah gave a half-hearted wave; she was feeling guilty for snapping at him by the Boating Centre. Instead of returning the wave, James dodged out of sight. He looked unmistakably shifty.

When Henry answered the door, he was all smiles – until he noticed their dad. He sized him up with narrowed eyes.

'So here you are, Kosmatka.' Henry coughed up the name as if he was allergic. 'What a surprise! Took your time, didn't you?'

Layah's dad gulped and turned pink.

Their mum started talking loudly about boats and picnic food and Henry swung back into the role of gallant host. He enlisted their mum to help him with the picnic hampers and Izzie dragged their dad away to investigate the Westwoods' library. Layah was left alone in the entrance hall. She glanced up at the grand staircase and, checking Henry wasn't in sight, she started to climb the stairs to the gallery above. The second floor was a honey-coloured corridor lined with long windows. Layah noticed a door was propped open and, feeling reckless, she marched in.

It was a fashionably boring office. The only interesting thing was a huge painting of a blue sky covered in golden hoops.

There was an 'Ouch!' to her right and Layah saw James emerging from a cupboard. He reddened when he saw her.

'What are you doing?' asked Layah.

'Nothing!' James protested. 'I – well, actually, I was looking for the keys to my Vespa. My father likes to hide them.'

'Need any help?'

James gave a nod-shrug, but Layah could tell he was pleased. He gestured to the giant desk and they set about searching it; James tackled the right set of drawers and Layah took the left. The drawers were full of folders marked *Confidential* and fancy pens in padded cases.

'So why does your dad hide your keys?' asked Layah, struggling to open a box of pearl cufflinks.

James flicked his dark fringe out of his eyes. For a second she thought he was going to tell her to mind her own business, but after a breath he said, 'He doesn't like me riding it – the Vespa – because it was a present from my mother. Just part of the fun of having divorced parents!'

'Oh.' Layah looked up. 'Does their divorce bother you?'

James paused. He sank down to sit on the carpet.

'It's all right.' He shrugged. 'I was eight when they

split. It's a lot quieter. Only now they really hate each other and don't bother hiding it.'

Layah sat down beside him, her back to the desk.

'Does your mum live near here?' she asked.

'No. My mother lives all over really – she's Jiya Jamal, the supermodel' – a glow of pride passed his face – 'which is cool, but she's busy most of the time. Her work comes first.'

'Sounds like my dad,' sighed Layah. 'He's always worked a lot but since my babcia died we hardly ever see him. It's like he's given up on us.' She dropped her gaze. 'My family is kind of messed up at the moment.'

'"Messed up" is my family motto.' James grinned. 'But your dad's here; at least he's making an effort.'

'For now,' mumbled Layah.

She didn't want to talk about her parents any more. The thought of them hating each other made her feel poisonous inside.

'So,' she said, 'how are you getting on with unmasking the Lowesdale Stranger?'

James's face cleared and he grinned.

'Well, actually, I was planning on doing some investigating today,' he said. 'I was going to ride out to the library – see if they've got any old newspaper articles

113

about the Stranger. You could come along, if you want?'

'I should probably stay with my family,' said Layah. 'Do you still think it's just some guy in the woods?'

'Yeah. They're definitely human!'

'Yes, but . . .' Layah chose her words carefully. 'I think there's some other stuff going on too.'

She thought about telling him what she knew – about the Midnight Visitor, and maybe even about L. Bellford. She still wasn't sure if he'd laugh at her. But it wasn't like Layah believed in Izzie's creature theory.

Before she could make up her mind, they heard her mum's voice in the corridor. The door burst open and her mum appeared; she looked breathless.

'Layah, stop running off!' chided Mum. 'What are you doing on the floor?'

'Found them!' James grabbed a set of keys and jumped up. 'I'd best go. I'll let you know what I find . . . I mean – enjoy the picnic! Um – catch you later.'

He scarpered. Layah's mum was gazing around the room, an odd expression on her face. Layah felt winded by James's sudden departure. Maybe she should have gone with him to the library. He looked so disappointed when she had refused.

'Shall we go, then?' Layah hoisted herself to her feet. 'Mum? What's wrong?'

Her mum was still standing there, frozen to the spot.

'I'm not feeling very well.' Her mum's voice quavered. 'I . . . I don't think I should go. I'm feeling rather faint.'

Layah stared at her. Her mum looked almost translucent; blue veins stood out like cobwebs in her white face.

'Are you OK?' said Layah cautiously.

'I'm fine.' Her mum lowered her eyes. 'I just need a moment. You go and have fun.'

Layah hesitated. She could ask her about L. Bellford, right now. She could demand the truth before it was too late and her mum had drifted even further away from her. But what if Layah asked and her mum lied again? Just like she had lied about the sleepwalking and the school. Layah turned away.

'Layah.'

She looked back expectantly.

'Tell the others and – take care of Izzie, out on the water, won't you?' Mum said softly. 'Take care of each other.'

The girl climbed up and up, her bag on her back, looking to the south. She had walked further than she had ever gone before. Twilight was falling and the mountainside was empty but for a solitary crow. Not many ramblers could climb as high as she did. Jagged rocks and mossy stumps signposted the path and fog lurked in the undergrowth. The girl gazed unseeing at the scurrying clouds. Her mind was churning. Cowardice had been her only option and it was worth it if it kept the three humans safe. She would not kill the innocent.

Then a noise made her stiffen. A slow whistling mingled with the fog – eerie and deadly.

'Thought you could run away and hide, did you?'

The girl whipped around and saw the Other stalking up the mountain path behind her. Black clouds rumbled on the horizon.

'Thought it would be easy to turn your back on who you are?'

The girl stumbled and her heel caught the edge of the cliff; grit tumbled down the ridge behind her.

'I can't do this.' The words spoke through her. 'I won't kill them. I don't want this—'

'You pity them?' sneered the Other. 'You deluded girl. They are not like us – they are different, strange, ignorant. They hate and fear powerful females. Do you know what they will do if they find you? They will slice you open like a rat and bottle your powers!'

The Other took a step towards her.

'At least they have a choice – they can choose who they want to be!' said the girl.

The Other gave a chilling laugh. A gust of wind shoved the girl backwards and she swayed on the edge.

'You foolish girl,' hissed the Other, 'you think choice is freedom? Power is freedom! We are their superiors.'

'Then why are you doing this?' cried the girl. 'Why kill them?'

'Because our mysteries must be protected with blood! I will spare no one who threatens our secrets!'

The wind screamed in agreement.

'What if we're making a mistake?' the girl yelled.

There was a boom of thunder, the crashing

symphony of a deadly storm. Hail began to fall like icicles.

There was a thud and a crow was forced from the sky by the wind and hit the rock beside the girl. The crow squeaked in pain, as if held by an invisible iron fist of wind. As the girl reached out to save it, the bird was swept over the clifftop and plummeted into the valley below.

The Other reached out and grabbed the girl by the throat; her feet left the mountain and she was dangling over the edge, kicking above the dizzying drop below.

'This is not the demeanour of a warrior,' the Other screamed. 'Where is your honour? Think of our ancestors! This task is a chance to prove yourself – to perform a noble deed – and instead you run to the mountains to hide. You are a coward.'

'I'll do it then!' the girl yelled, her toes reaching for the rock. 'I promise! I won't be weak!'

'Then prove it!'

The Other released her hand from the girl's throat and the girl dropped, the wind and rain rushing up to meet her. She screamed, squeezed her eyes shut, then, suddenly – she soared upwards into the sky, calling to the crows.

# Chapter Thirteen

Layah's dad and Henry stood at opposite ends of the Westwoods' private jetty, Henry with his arms behind his back, surveying his estate with smug satisfaction, the sun glinting off his blonde head. Their dad looked small and ragged by comparison.

Layah and Izzie were sitting aboard the Vellamo speedboat, swaying in the water.

'When Ren said a boat, I thought she meant a real boat, not this waterborne sea-car!' mumbled Dad, his face growing pinker. 'What about that one over there?'

He pointed at a Wayfarer which had been dragged up on to the grass and lay in the sunlight, its paint peeling. It had the shadowed word *Jiya* printed on its side.

'This is a man's boat, Kosmatka,' scoffed Henry. 'That wreck isn't fit for water. You'll take the boat or get out. Catch.' The keys landed on the deck with a clatter. 'She can be tricky in high winds; I do hope you don't take a tumble. Bon voyage.' And he strode back towards the house.

Their dad clambered down into the boat, muttering darkly. 'A man's boat . . . a toddler could drive this thing.'

It was a full five minutes until their dad managed to find the ignition switch. After a rumbling start, the Vellamo began to glide into the centre of the lake.

Layah leant over the back and watched the blue-white water churn out behind them. She was still thinking about her mum. What had made her change her mind like that? Was it something to do with Henry? Would she rather spend more time with Henry than her own family? Whatever the reason, her mum certainly wasn't sick.

'You all right, girls?' called Dad, flapping open a map. 'Avery Island here we come, eh!'

'I didn't realise we were going to the island,' Layah said sharply.

'Thought it would be a nice idea,' Dad shouted over the engine.

The haunting feeling the island had brought out in Layah came flooding back as the boat picked up speed.

'What do you reckon?' Layah whispered to Izzie.

'We might find some more clues,' said Izzie. 'More

feathers, perhaps?'

'I'm sure you'll find lots of feathers – from *birds*, that is!' scoffed Layah.

'"Be prepared for the impossible." That's what Babcia would say,' said Izzie sagely. 'Anyway, look what I found in the Westwoods' library.' She extracted a book from her rucksack. 'They must have thousands of books and it just so happens they had this one.'

Layah recognised it at once: *Tales from Ancient Poland: Songs of Kings and Monsters* by Professor Ana Kosmatka.

'Babcia's book of ancient poems!' exclaimed Layah. 'You want to read the poem about the king and the monster, don't you?'

'Page 124.' Izzie nodded as Layah turned the pages.

'I still don't know how helpful this is,' muttered Layah. 'It might just have been a coincidence Mr Speckleback mentioning "shapeshifting fiends".'

Still, Layah opened to the poem and Izzie squished on to the bench beside her.

The poem was one of the oldest discoveries in the book. Babcia had found the manuscript in an ancient burial ground, lost in a tangled forest between Poland and Belarus. No one knew who had written the poem – it had been wrapped in leather, half-rotten after thousands of years. Layah had seen the original manuscript at the university in Krakow, cracked parchment speckled with a forgotten language which had taken Babcia years to translate.

Layah and Izzie bent over the book and read together:

'King Vukasin and Mandalina'
Translation from Old Polish


*Lean in! To hear a tale of dark misdeeds.*
*A cunning foe – a villainess – draws near . . .*
*Released from myth, she prowls with feathered tread.*
*Mistrust her human face – monster she does be.*

*Meet our hero brave King Vukasin,*
*Who sought a force to keep his kingdom great.*
*Fate led him, set him searching, to a glen.*
*There a war-maid, with might unmastered, slept.*

*Hushed, he crept to steal her spell-bound helmet.*
*When she awoke, he staked his claim, his right*
*He knew, whoever thieved her helmet so*
*She must obey, submit her will to his.*

*For many suns, she fought with guts and grit,*

*Upheld his law, in blooded battles won.*
*And King, love-blind for his faithful fighter,*
*Gave back the helmet – which bound her soul to him.*

*Free! Gruesome, gross, shapeshifting fiend, she was!*
*Her heinous cry did moult her maiden skin.*
*Beneath a grim, black-winged beast revealed,*
*Revenge and plunder in its blazing eyes.*

*Quick-footed King, leapt, snatched up her bow.*
*(Only weapon took from her heathen grasp*
*Could have smote that creature's life to dust.)*
*He struck! Shot he the fierce deceiver dead.*

*Glory, balance and order new restored.*
*From mortal lands must evil taint be purged.*

'I forgot what a pompous pig that King Vukasin was,' said Layah, 'he's supposed to be this brave hero but he still needs someone else to fight his battles for him.'

'Babcia said all kings were pompous pigs in those days,' agreed Izzie. 'She said it was part of the job description.'

Layah smiled. It had been Babcia's voice reading the poem in her head.

'The creature in the poem,' said Izzie, '*a grim, black-winged beast* – it's kind of like a bird-woman, isn't it? Just like Mr Speckleback was talking about.'

'Well . . .' Layah was reluctant. 'Yes, the feathers after the attack were weird but there could be loads of reasons . . . maybe the feathers were a trick to scare us and distract us from the L. Bellford mystery. Maybe the person who attacked me was wearing a sort of costume.'

'I think the poem has something to do with the mystery of the feathers,' said Izzie firmly, as she put the book back into her rucksack.

Layah wasn't sure what to say – she felt bad, but they couldn't jump to any conclusions.

With Westwood Manor far behind them, the lake and the sky opened up around them and the Vellamo sped like a razor blade across the water towards Avery Island. It peaked up from the lake like a dark green volcano; a jagged rockface encircled most of the perimeter so it was only safe to land on one side, where the slope was smooth and grassy. There was no sign of any birds darting above the trees, but that didn't mean they weren't lurking out of sight.

The Vellamo bumped gently into the small jetty and their dad jumped on to the wet boards, dragging the rope round a hook and knotting it securely. He looked up at the hill, blinking in the sun.

'You talk to Dad,' whispered Izzie as she clambered unsteadily out of the boat. 'Ask him whether Mum has ever mentioned an L. Bellford. I'll suss out the island.'

'What?' stammered Layah. 'No, you talk to him. He doesn't want to talk to me.'

'Layah. I think you're being silly,' said Izzie. 'You've hardly spoken to him since he arrived.'

Layah couldn't escape the look Izzie gave her – like she was peering into a hidden corner of Layah's heart.

'But, Iz . . .' Layah squirmed. 'I can't let you go off alone. What if the attacker is on the island?'

'It's the middle of the day. I'll be fine.' Izzie smiled. 'This is important.'

Layah knew Izzie had a point.

'You girls going to help carry the picnic?' called Dad, wobbling under the weight of three hampers.

'Dad, Layah will help,' replied Izzie, reminding Layah irresistibly of Mum when she was organising them for school. 'I'm going off to look around.'

'Oh well . . . OK,' he said, looking nervously at Layah. 'Just don't go too close to the water.'

'I won't. See you in a bit.'

Izzie set off up the hillside and Layah watched her

disappear, wondering when her sister had grown so confident. *It's the middle of the day,* she repeated to herself, *and she won't be far away.*

# Chapter Fourteen

Layah and her dad set up the picnic site without speaking. The hampers were full of china crockery, silver cutlery and parcels of cold meats, sausage rolls, cheese scones, vegetable tarts and salad with strips of chicken. The smallest hamper contained the desserts: apple and cinnamon muffins and fruit salad and cream.

Layah sat on a corner of the mat, laying out the cups and saucers. Her dad seemed a little nervous around her and Layah felt a pang of regret. She missed how they used to be together.

'Oh, he didn't spare any expense, did he?' sighed Dad, peering into the basket. 'Is that cold pheasant? Blimey! I see Henry's the same arrogant guy he was at school.'

'Mum seems to like him,' said Layah quietly.

She saw her dad's face drop and felt instantly guilty. Why was her instinct always to push people away?

She looked out at the empty lake. The village was

out of sight around the bend but she could still see the peak of the Lowesdale Giant dark against the sky.

'Um, Dad,' Layah began awkwardly, 'you know that poem . . . "King Vukasin and Mandalina"?'

He nodded, pushing his glasses up his nose. 'Your babcia's most famous translation,' he said. 'I wanted to read it at the funeral but the youngest brother's job is to arrange the flowers. And I do know a lot about flowers but . . . it would have been nice.'

'Well, um . . .' Layah couldn't believe she was asking this! 'Could a shapeshifting fiend with black wings and blazing eyes actually exist? A kind of bird-woman? Could they be real?'

'Real?' Her dad chuckled. 'Oh no! Well, technically some hybrid species are possible – ever heard of a liger? Or was it a tion . . .? Anyway! A tiger-lion hybrid has been created but not a human-bird hybrid; that would be too complicated. The "shapeshifting fiend" in the poem will be a metaphor for something, I expect. Ask your mum about that, she's much cleverer than me. She's smart and funny and radiant . . .' His voice faded away sadly.

'Right,' Layah ploughed on. 'Dad, have you ever heard Mum talk about anyone called L. Bellford? Apart from me, I mean, or has she ever said anything about any of her Bellford family?'

But her dad didn't seem to be listening any more; he was staring out over the silvery lake.

'You know, it was all because of Henry that your mum and I met,' he sighed. 'If he hadn't thrown that party . . . it was a celebration for the rugby team – I was only there because Henry wanted to copy my biology homework – but then, I met your mum in the queue for the toilet. I was too nervous to speak, but she suddenly looked at me and said, "Looks like we're stuck here, we might as well get to know each other,"' he said, with a faint smile.

Layah knew the story better than the poem, her dad had told them so many times. Her parents had met when they were fifteen. Layah couldn't imagine her parents as teenagers!

'She was so beautiful,' Dad mumbled, 'cleverest person I'd ever met, besides your babcia, of course.'

'So why are you messing everything up now? Why are you never around any more?' The words burst from her. 'Since Babcia died – you've just given up on us!'

Her dad stared down at his cup. 'I'm a disappointment, aren't I?' he said.

'You don't need to be,' sighed Layah.

Her dad looked at her, his eyes hopeful. 'Layah, my

work isn't simple. It's difficult to get time off and—'

A scream pierced through the air.

They both twisted around to see Izzie pelting down the hillside, calling something which was lost in the wind. Layah sprang to her feet and, as Izzie sprinted closer, she made out the word she was shouting:

'RUN!'

Layah looked up into the sky and saw them.

For a second, she might have called them bats. They had the twirling movement of bats, but she knew what they were: crows. Forty or fifty of them. Sharp-beaked and with powerful wings, they whirled through the air like a tornado, swooping over the island; they began to corkscrew towards them.

'Layah! Dad! Run!' Izzie screamed again, her amber necklace swinging violently as she thundered towards them.

Layah reacted first and was already bolting towards the boat, calling back to her dad, who had frozen in horror.

'Dad! Come on!' Layah shrieked.

Izzie rammed into him, grabbing his sleeve, and dragged him along the jetty after Layah. The sunny afternoon had been broken by a sudden violent storm; rain sliced down in shards as her dad and Izzie trampled towards the boat.

'Dad. Let's go!' Layah cried, scrabbling to untie the mooring rope.

Leaping on to the Vellamo, her dad grabbed the wheel, fumbling with the keys.

'The key! The engine! It's not starting!' he yelled, thumping the dashboard.

'Dad! Come on! Just make it work!' demanded Layah, jumping down into the boat and turning the keys with him.

*Don't look round. Don't look round.* The words were thudding in Layah's head. Then Izzie screamed again and Layah turned. The crows were seconds from them, cruel claws arched as their feathers were tossed up in the whirlwind which seemed to be carrying them forward.

'We've got to move!' shouted Izzie.

'Izzie, get down! Now!'

Layah darted to her sister, grabbed her shoulder, trying to pull her on to the deck.

'We've got to move!' Izzie cried again, hitting the edge of the boat with her fist.

A tremendous wave suddenly rolled below the Vellamo and the boat shot forward, propelled by the water. Spray cascaded over the sides, as if two white hands of foam were pushing the boat away from the island. Both sisters slipped and fell, clutching each other. Layah sat up and stared back.

The lake was furious beneath them; giant waves crashed in their slipstream, pushing the boat further out. A great wind seemed to rise from the lake itself. Layah's hair scattered across her face as she looked up into the sky, dark with feathers. The crows seemed to have lost their formation; their shrieks were hair-raisingly human. The birds were being battered about by a new rush of wind, weaving helplessly in the spray from the waves.

The Vellamo howled as the engine vibrated and the boat forged through the water. The birds were wheeling back to the island.

Layah staggered towards her sister and wrapped an arm around her.

'You're soaked,' Layah shouted above the engine. 'Here! Get this on.' She tugged the picnic blanket around Izzie's shoulders.

'I'm all right, Layah,' panted Izzie, 'you need to get warm too!'

They both looked back at the island. It was shrinking in the distance, a gloomy silhouette with the crows circling above it like flies. Layah was struggling to accept it but she knew that wasn't normal bird behaviour. Something unnatural was going on. And if the birds weren't normal, then – she hated to admit it – perhaps neither was their mystery.

# CHAPTER FIFTEEN

That had been a narrow escape. The triumphant relief which had flooded Layah started to drain away as she, Izzie and their dad stumbled back up the lawn towards Westwood Manor. Behind them, the lake was serene once more but grey clouds obscured the sky like smoke. There was an unnatural chill in the air, as if the whole of Lowesdale was holding its breath.

The back door to the Manor was unlocked and the house was filled with a gentle hush. There was no sign of James, Henry or their mum. Their dad left them in the entrance hall and went off to find the others.

'What happened?' Layah asked, the moment their dad had gone.

'I just went for a walk through the trees,' said Izzie; her fingers were almost blue with cold. 'I found a tunnel. I wasn't going to go in. I thought maybe it was for a fox or . . . and then I saw them coming up from inside.'

134

'The birds came from inside the tunnel?' asked Layah.

'Yes.' Izzie took a shuddering breath. 'As soon as I saw them, I knew they were coming for us. Like they'd been ordered to attack us.'

'Yeah. Well, birds can be trained,' said Layah quickly. 'Let's think practically about this. They can also get mad bird disease and go crazy.'

'I think that's just cows.'

'Whatever. We'll work out what's going on,' said Layah firmly.

She was trying to calm herself as much as Izzie, who was still shivering. Unlike Layah, who had her coat, Izzie had only been wearing a jumper, and had been utterly drenched.

'Layah, if you want to find out who L. Bellford is you need to go to Newbeck now,' said Izzie. 'Tomorrow might be too late. We might be going back to London.'

'But – but I can't go without you,' gasped Layah. 'And right now, you need to get warm and drink a pint of hot chocolate!'

'Yes, you can,' said Izzie, taking off her rucksack. 'Take the photograph, go to Newbeck, to Wickerberry Cottage on Primrose Street and find Mistress Brown. I'll cover for you, with Dad.'

'You're sure you'll be all right?'

'Layah! Go!'

Layah slung Izzie's rucksack over her shoulders and then slipped through the front door. She hurried down the driveway, feeling the windows of the house watching her like giant eyes. She jogged down the lane to Rook Cottage. The cottage looked empty and Layah grabbed her bike and swerved down the road towards Lowesdale. She was lucky; a tatty two-decker reached the bus stop just as Layah was locking up Henry's bike. As Layah took her seat, she glanced out of the window, and saw a distant figure by the lakeside: Mor Hemlock, surrounded by a flock of hungry seagulls. Layah leant back and the bus jerked out on to the open road.

The familiar village of Lowesdale was soon a long-forgotten signpost as the bus sped along deserted roads; the top deck swayed dangerously as it rounded corners and yoyo-ed over hills. Field after field of bored sheep flashed outside as Layah hunched in her seat at the back, hoping she didn't look like a lost kid. Her fellow passengers were a group of walkers, who were all sharing a large bag of carrot sticks, and took no notice of Layah.

Where had her mum and Henry disappeared to? Was their disappearance connected to the bird attack? It seemed too much of a coincidence . . .

Thoughts of crows, ancient poems and L. Bellford

were all mushing together in Layah's head. She thought of Mor Hemlock – the person the villagers said was helping the Lowesdale Stranger. Was she honestly starting to believe that there was a shapeshifting winged monster running around Lowesdale? Could the woman with yellow eyes really be something other than human? When Babcia had translated the Mandalina poem, had she ever wondered, just for a moment, whether the beast – the 'war-maid' Mandalina – could possibly have been real?

Layah touched her amber pendant. Izzie and she had always admired the precious stones which Babcia had kept in a black box on her desk. When they were small, Babcia would place a pendant in each of their hands and take them to the window, to watch the amber glint from fiery orange to deep gold.

'It's magic!' Izzie would always gasp.

'No! It's the sunlight,' Layah would explain.

Then Babcia would smile. 'Sunlight can be magical. You know, girls, in ancient Poland, amber was considered lucky – people believed that its brightness would keep away dark forces.'

Layah had never properly considered why Babcia had left them the necklaces. She thought it was simply a beautiful gift. Had Babcia truly believed the amber was lucky? And what dark forces were they supposed to protect them from?

An hour later, at Newbeck, Layah followed the walkers off the bus. She left the car park and walked up the hill, passing the Royal Lark Hotel. It wasn't until she reached the high street that she realised she had no idea where she was supposed to go. The map wasn't working on her phone and she felt utterly useless without it.

Newbeck was bigger than Lowesdale and was packed with bustling holidaymakers. The town centre was jammed with bed and breakfasts, shops selling tourist gifts – authentic Newbeck thimbles and 'fish-flavoured' fudge – and there was a parade of tea rooms, all owned by a string of Bettys, Marys and Aunt Dollys.

Foggy panic turned to desperation, so Layah paused outside an old-fashioned sweetshop. The window was lined with multicoloured sweets in glass jars. Pulling herself together, Layah entered the shop. She bought a sugar mouse for Izzie and asked where she might find Primrose Street and soon Layah was, gratefully, on her way.

Primrose Street was a sleepy road with neat flowerbeds and clean brick bungalows. It seemed safe enough, but Layah couldn't help looking furtively behind her as she rang the doorbell of Wickerberry Cottage.

The elderly lady who appeared had a round face like

a Persian cat, white whiskery eyebrows and pale pink lipstick.

'Mistress Brown?' asked Layah, feeling like a small child.

'Hello, love. Do I know you? You from the grocer's?' The old lady squinted up at Layah.

'Um . . . no. I'm . . . I wanted to ask you about Lowesdale School – about an old pupil.'

'Oh. You got family at Lowesdale, eh?'

At the mention of the school, Ms Brown opened the door wider and beckoned Layah forward. She gestured Layah towards the living room, which was a web of white doilies and faded velvet. Ms Brown settled on to an armchair and pointed to the sofa opposite.

'Just plonk yourself down, duck, and let me know how I can help you,' said Ms Brown, smiling easily. 'Always happy to help out old girls and their little 'uns.'

Now she was here Layah's confidence faltered. It all seemed so ludicrously serious to be sitting here in the light of day in this little old lady's cottage. What would Izzie do? She wished her sister was with her. Layah took out the photo of the tennis team and slid the frame across the coffee table.

'My sister and I found this photo,' explained Layah, 'and we were wondering if you could tell us about it.

Is that you?'

Ms Brown's face shone with memory as she studied it. 'Oh yes. That was me. Bless those white dresses! I remember that year so well.' She ran a finger over her likeness. 'Oh goodness, it takes me back! Yes, we won the silver cup – the Cumbrian Schoolgirls' Tennis Championships.' She looked up at Layah curiously. 'Who did you say your mother was, duck? Sandra Sanderson, was it?'

'Um . . . I wanted to know about this girl.' Layah pointed. 'L. Bellford. I was wondering if you knew where she was now? See, I think we might be related or something and I thought . . .'

The old lady's face turned grey. 'Is this a joke?' whispered Ms Brown. 'Are you from the newspapers?'

'What? No . . . I . . . I'm sorry, I just wanted to know about . . . L. Bellford.'

'Lauren?' Ms Brown's voice cracked as she said the name.

'Laur— Mum?' Layah gasped. 'Lauren? Do you mean Ren? Ren Bellford? This is a photo of Ren Bellford? I don't understand; Mum went to school in London. She didn't . . .'

'Lauren Mary Bellford,' whispered Ms Brown with a feeble nod.

Mum? All this time L. Bellford had been her mum? Layah felt like she'd been slapped across the face.

'I don't understand.' Layah blinked across at Ms Brown. 'Lauren Mary Bellford is my mum. She – she never told us she went here. Did she grow up in Lowesdale?'

'Your . . . mum?'

Ms Brown clutched at her chest, her eyes round as pound coins.

'Yes, she's our mum. Can you tell me more about her at school? Why did she move to London?' asked Layah. 'Do you know anything about her parents?'

Slowly Ms Brown rose to her feet and shuffled to the bookshelf. She brought back a thick scrapbook and opened it to reveal a flutter of papers and photographs. She shifted through it and held out a newspaper cutting.

Still confused, Layah took it and read the headline:

# FIRE AT SWEETSHOP

*Death and tragedy at Frank and Janet Bellford's sweetshop last night after a freak fire destroyed their shop and home.*

Layah looked up at Ms Brown.

141

'A fire? Her parents? Were they killed?' Layah felt a cold sadness spreading over her. 'So these were my grandparents? Mum never said . . .'

'No, love,' Ms Brown quailed, 'Lauren Bellford . . . oh dear, do you have anyone I can call for you?'

'What?' Layah stared. 'What do you mean? What happened after this fire?'

'That's just it, love,' the old lady's face was ghoulish with fear, 'she – Lauren – died in that fire with her parents when she was thirteen years old.'

Layah felt the page of newsprint slip from her hand. There was a strange buzzing in her ears. She didn't understand.

'OK,' Layah said slowly, 'maybe there's been a mistake. Lauren Mary Bellford is my mum. Look, I can show you!'

Layah pulled out her phone. She scrolled through her photos and found one of her mum, her hair tumbling out of her butterfly clip and her wide smile perfectly captured. Layah turned the photo to Ms Brown. The old lady took the phone like it was a glass ornament. A shudder passed over her face and she looked away.

'What's wrong?' demanded Layah. 'This is Lauren. She's alive.'

'It must be that girl,' whispered Ms Brown. 'It was

142

the morning after the fire. Mr Onbury had offered to make me a cup of tea. We knew that there was no hope. Frank, Janet and poor Lauren were gone. I was standing by the window when I saw the girl in the street. She looked so much like dear Lauren that I nearly screamed. I watched her. And as she passed by, I saw she was wearing Lauren's school coat, toggled up and school crest showing . . . And I knew an evil changeling had come to threaten our sweet town. Why do you bring these terrible memories back to haunt me? Who are you?'

'Who was that other girl? What did you actually see?' said Layah.

'I saw the eyes of a monster in that changeling girl – the girl in Lauren's coat.' Ms Brown choked, tears on her powdery cheeks. 'The shining yellow eyes of a monster.'

Layah stood up, her heartbeat pounding in her head. If L. Bellford had died in a fire, then had the girl in her coat been Layah's mum? A girl with yellow eyes. But if her mum had never truly been Lauren Mary Bellford, then who was she?

'I'm sorry to have upset you,' said Layah, 'but I need to go. I need to get back to my sister.'

Layah was staggering from the room before she had finished speaking. She flung open the front door and ran.

The charred shell of the shop was like a house made of bones. The dull morning light was grey and dirty-white. Inside the shop, the sweets, the garish wallpaper, the gold scales had all been drained of colour.

The street outside was deserted. A graveyard hour. Stiller and emptier than the moment the flames had first sparked into life. That was several hours ago now. The screaming fire truck, the ambulance, the hysterical neighbours, they had all come and gone. Life had come and gone. And now it was nearing the break of yet another silent morning.

Above the shop – the flat where the family had lived – a chill breeze trickled across the floor, fanning the pages of a fallen book.

The girl stepped carefully along the peeling floorboards. It was like stepping along the gangway of a ship.

She turned her glowing yellow eyes about the room. The police were yet to inspect it. They had been ordered back to the station with the promise of sausage sandwiches. 'No rush, lads. There's nothing we can do now.'

The girl picked her way into the second bedroom. Three walls were intact but the fourth was open to the sky. Black coal-covered posters, photos and school timetables still hung to the three remaining walls.

'You have impressed me.'

The girl turned, blinking her yellow eyes back to hazel.

'This is what you wanted?' she said dully.

'Of course,' said the Other, 'we have killed the threat – those snooping Bellfords! They will not trouble us any more. Are you not pleased? You have proven yourself. Your foremothers would be proud. Do you not feel their strength within you?'

The girl's face was empty. She looked around at the skeleton of the room, once a home and now rubble.

'I understand now,' said the girl, 'I will always be stronger than the humans. The power I have . . . it will always set me apart. We are invincible, but we must always be invisible.'

'We are superior!' purred the Other. 'They are useless beings.'

'Then I know what I have to do.'

The girl held out the gold bracelet she had found on the forest floor. The Other began to laugh, a harsh mocking cackle which rose with the dirty smoke. The girl stood and waited.

# CHAPTER SIXTEEN

Layah fumbled with her mobile and found Izzie's number. It rang, rang, rang without answer until the answerphone responded.

'Izzie I'm coming back! I've just seen Ms Brown and I'm freaking out a bit. L. Bellford is Mum – only she's dead! Mum stole the real L. Bellford's identity. I know it sounds mad, but I'm scared. We can't trust her. You need to call me!'

She stuffed her phone back in her pocket. The bus stop was on the other side of town and she didn't know when the next one was due to arrive. Dread was freezing her insides as she ran. If their mum wasn't who they thought she was – why had she lied to them? Was this the reason she had come to the Lakes? To shed her fake identity and rid herself of the lousy husband and tiresome kids and return to who she was before? But who was that? *What* was that?

There was a loud honk and the bus trundled past.

Layah hurtled down the high street; she burst between a kissing couple and leapt over dog leads. She tore into the car park just in time to see the bus disappearing down the main road. The next bus wouldn't arrive for another two hours. Layah kicked up a spray of grit, then she fumbled for her phone again – no answer from Izzie – she had never felt so helpless.

'Oi! Layah!'

Layah whirled around and saw James in his leather jacket. She flew towards him; he recoiled, as if worried she was going to hit him, and she seized his sleeve.

'James! I need to get back to Rook Cottage as fast as possible. Can I have a ride?'

'Why? What's wrong?' He stared at her. 'What are you doing here?'

'Not now – I need to get back!'

'This way.' He hurried towards his waiting Vespa. 'I've just been to the Newbeck Library – and I found an old newspaper article about the Lowesdale Stranger!'

'Sounds great – but can we go?'

'Don't worry, we'll get there.' He was unlocking the seat of the Vespa. 'But Layah, I was wrong – the stories about the Lowesdale Stranger only started about forty years ago. And I never knew they discovered a hideout in the forest: a cottage built into the mountainside. That was about twenty-seven years ago and there haven't been any new sightings of the Stranger since!'

It was twenty-seven years since her mum – Lauren Bellford – had won a scholarship for a school in London, thought Layah, her mind whirring. Twenty-seven years since the fire in the sweetshop.

James pulled out a second helmet and handed it over.

'Put this on, and this.' He pulled off his jacket and gave it to her. 'Have you ever been on a scooter before?'

'No!' she said, staring wild-eyed at him. 'Of course not.'

'All you need to do is hold on.'

'And you're sure you can ride?' said Layah, wobbling on to the back. 'I mean, you've had lessons and all that?'

He grinned, swinging his leg over the seat.

'I've been driving a car since I was eleven; I got my first scooter when I was thirteen. Trust me, I'm getting you back in one piece.'

The Vespa tore off down the country road. Layah felt like she was on a rocket; the green and blue countryside liquidated into one long spiral of sound and speed.

It took forty minutes to get to Lowesdale, but Layah

had no sense of time any more.

As they whipped round a bend, she caught sight of two people – a man and a small girl – walking up the hill.

'James! Stop!' Layah called.

The Vespa rolled to a halt just as the track to Rook Cottage was coming into sight ahead. Layah twisted off and unclipped the helmet.

'Thank you, James!'

'Should I stay?' he asked, eagerly.

'No – I just need to talk to Izzie. But thank you!'

She ran back down the road and the Vespa zoomed away behind her.

'Izzie! Dad!'

Layah collided with Izzie, hugged her, then gripped her at arm's length.

'Did you hear my message?' panted Layah.

'Yes.' Izzie nodded, her face flushed. 'We still haven't seen Mum. She wasn't at the Manor. Dad and I went to the Boat Café – to stock up on sugar. Where has she gone?'

'Maybe she knows we know,' said Layah frantically. 'Maybe she's going to run!'

Layah raced back up the hill, dragging Izzie along with her, their dad chasing behind them.

'Wait up, you two!' he puffed.

'Layah, look!' Izzie pointed.

The top window on the right – the window of their mum's bedroom – had the curtains drawn and a flickering light danced behind them.

'We've got to confront her,' said Layah firmly. 'Even if it's . . . it's dangerous.'

A few days ago, she wouldn't have thought to connect danger with her own mum but now it didn't seem so far-fetched. The cottage door was locked and bolted. Their dad knocked and called but there was no answer. The light from the bedroom was unmistakably firelight. What was she doing in there?

'I think your mum must be asleep,' said Dad, scratching his head. 'Or maybe she's in the bath.'

'We should go around the back,' said Layah to Izzie. 'There must be a way!'

They rushed to the back of the cottage, leapt over their mum's handmade tripwire (their dad tumbled behind them), and found the kitchen door locked too. Layah looked around the garden, then strode over to the bare washing line pole and tugged it out of the earth.

'Wow! Layah! What do you think you're doing?' exclaimed Dad. 'I'm sure Ren will hear us in a—'

Layah spun the pole about and jabbed it into one of

the panels in the glass door. It shattered and her dad gave a little yelp.

'Layah! For goodness' sake!'

'I'm sorry, Dad, but we need to get inside.'

Izzie handed Layah her jumper and Layah rolled it around her hand. She pushed the spikes of glass out of the frame, reached inside and managed to pull back the new silver bolt.

'We've got to push it,' Layah commanded.

'Dad, come on!' called Izzie.

Looking utterly befuddled, their dad added his weight to the door. The three of them slammed into it and the door finally sprang open.

'Henry's not going to be happy about this . . .' mumbled Dad, although Layah could hear the glee in his voice.

The girls hurried past him and stopped at the foot of the stairs, looking up at the shadowy landing.

'Iz, stay behind me,' said Layah and she advanced up the stairs, the pole from the washing line still in her hands.

'It's Mum,' cried Izzie. 'She's not dangerous.'

They were on the landing now and could see the light squirming below their mum's bedroom door. There was a strange rasping noise coming from inside. Layah held the pole in front of her and moved slowly forward. She could feel Babcia's amber pendant, warm against her skin. In a sudden movement Layah kicked the bedroom door open, wielding the pole like a spear. The room beyond burst into sight. Layah saw the candles, their flames shivering in the draught, their mum standing with her back to them facing the mirror. Beyond her, the bulging yellow eyes and craggy face of the Midnight Visitor stared out from the reflection.

'I knew it!' shouted Layah. 'You liar!'

'Layah, no!' shouted Izzie.

'She doesn't care about us, Izzie! Her and the Midnight Visitor! They're working together!'

Layah charged the pole forward but their mum's hand shot out and tuged it out of Layah's grip. Layah tripped forward and smashed into the chest of drawers. Their mum turned and Izzie screamed. Their mum's face was transformed: her eyes were yellow and unlidded and her slender neck was elongated.

The creature, so like their mum but at the same time strangely distorted, gazed across at them. It was hunched and wild, like an animal ready to pounce.

'Iz, she's not right! Run!' yelled Layah, backing into the wall.

There was a horrible screeching and Layah saw the

woman in the mirror laughing, her mouth a hideous gaping hole.

'Mum?' Izzie gasped.

The creature's hands took a firmer grip of the pole and she stepped towards Izzie.

'No! Please!' Layah yelled. 'Don't hurt her!'

Their mum's body twisted round and the point of the pole hit the mirror, which shattered. A gust of air burst from the glass, extinguishing the candles. The woman's image vanished in a hundred shards and their mum collapsed on to the bed. Their dad crashed into the room, catching Izzie round the shoulders as he skidded to a stop.

'Ren! What's going on? What's all—' He pulled their mum round and Layah saw her mum's face, beautiful and familiar. Her eyelids fluttered and she opened her hazel eyes, looking dazed. Layah snatched up the pole and pointed it at her.

'Don't move.'

'Layah! What are you doing?' said Dad, batting the pole away. 'Ouch!'

'Dad. Get away. Don't touch her,' Layah said, prodding him.

Her mum rose to her feet, rubbing her face.

'Layah . . .' she started.

'No. I don't know what you are, but you're not our mum,' said Layah, dragging Izzie behind her. 'Dad, get away from it.'

'Layah, it's still me,' said Mum, tears dazzling her eyes.

'You're not even human,' cried Layah. 'You're plotting with that other thing. You're trying to trick us!'

Her dad was slumped on the floor, looking bewildered.

'Layah. I need you to understand who I am,' said Mum firmly. 'Please put that down.'

'Layah,' said Izzie, gently placing a hand on Layah's arm. 'I think we should listen to her.'

'No!' Layah's voice cracked; her own tears were falling now. 'No. Whatever she is, she's been lying to us for years.'

'Yes,' said Mum softly, 'but now I'm going to tell you the truth. I promise. Layah, I need you to listen to me because right now all of us are in danger. Mesula is on her way.'

# Chapter Seventeen

Dusk was settling, the colours in the garden fading from emerald to jade green. Lowesdale murmured with nestling wings, scurrying paws and sleepy eyes. Trees stretched their shadowed fingers across the lawn and a robin danced over the darkening flower beds.

In their mum's bedroom, Izzie and their dad sat on the bed, both holding large mugs of hot chocolate. Layah was pacing the floorboards, glaring at her mum, who sat on the window seat, her large purple jumper making her look smaller than usual.

'So?' Layah shot at her mum. 'How can we ever trust you again?'

'Layah . . .' Mum sighed, 'you're right. I am different. That woman and I . . . we are the same – um – species.'

'Species?'

Their dad had not stopped gawping since he had burst into the bedroom twenty minutes before. His eyes were popping out of his head and his hands were shaking so much there was hot chocolate leaking over his trousers.

'People have called us many things,' Mum explained. 'Valkyrie, Rusalka, shapeshifters – but these are one and the same. We are Vilsestra.'

The word seemed to shimmer in the silence.

'Vilsestra?' Dad whimpered finally.

Layah stood firm, arms folded and eyes narrowed.

'You're like the creature from that poem? "King Vukasin and Mandalina"?' demanded Layah.

'Yes.' Her mum nodded. 'In ancient times, when there were more Vilsestra, some poets did write about us. We are the descendants of goddesses and ancient birds with powers over the natural world – weather, sea and sky. We can communicate with birds through whistling or birdsong. We can hide our Vilsestra forms and retain human appearances – wings can be pretty inconvenient, I can tell you!' Their mum gave a small smile before clearing her throat seriously. 'Mesula believes Vilsestra are the superior species and wouldn't think twice about killing a human.'

Layah and Izzie shared a look. Izzie seemed surprisingly calm, more curious than shocked, but Layah was boiling with the unfairness of the lie. How could their mum have kept this secret from her own family?

'And how are you any different to this Mesula, *Mum*?' Layah spoke sarcastically and her mum flinched.

'Layah, I am still your mum. I ran away from Mesula twenty-seven years ago when I was thirteen years old. And until a week ago I thought I was free.'

'So what were you doing in the garden? I saw you! The night after the attack,' said Layah. 'Were you meeting her? This Mesula?'

'I've been trying to protect you,' pleaded Mum. 'After you saw her in the garden, I decided to sleep downstairs and do regular patrols of the cottage at night. I knew it was only a matter of time before she came again.'

'So is that why we left London?' asked Izzie from the bed. 'She found you?'

Her mum hung her head.

'It was the morning we left for Lowesdale,' she said solemnly. 'I saw her watching our house. I knew, if I had any chance of standing up to her, I needed to return to the Lakes. I think she wants to punish me for deserting her all those years ago.'

'What about Henry?' said Layah sharply.

'Henry had been bothering me about visiting for

158

months. I called him, asked him if we could stay in the cottage; I told him that your dad and I needed some time apart . . . which wasn't a complete lie.'

Her mum's eyes lingered on her husband and he gaped wordlessly back.

'It was a mistake to bring you,' continued Mum. 'If your dad hadn't been at the conference, he could have looked after you – and I couldn't leave you with friends, it would be too difficult to explain. Part of me wanted to keep you close, to protect you! I was wrong. I panicked and . . . I'm sorry. Bringing you here was too dangerous.'

'But why did you need to come to the Lakes?' asked Izzie gently.

Their mum paused, then rolled up her sleeve to reveal a gold bracelet; the initials L.B. were engraved on the band.

'Lauren Bellford,' breathed Layah. 'You stole her identity! She died in a fire. What happened to her? What did you do?'

Their mum was silent for a few moments.

'I didn't have the same choices as you,' Mum whispered. 'All I knew was Mesula. I was hidden away from the outside world; away from humans. You see, Mesula found me when I was born – well, technically,

159

I should say hatched . . .'

Layah gulped. She would never look at scrambled eggs in the same way again.

Their mum seemed to be gathering her strength; at last she spoke. 'I need to tell you a story,' she said, 'a story about a girl – a Vilsestra – who grew up in the care of a monster. We lived in the forest on the Lowesdale Giant. The Vilsestra have always lived in wild places. In ancient times, we were warriors commanding great swathes of wild land across Europe. Mesula clung to the ancient Teachings, to the stories and songs. As the last survivors of a dwindling clan, our secrecy was all we had. We had a hideout deep in the forest which Mesula had built. I was a secret. I was never allowed to go into the village, even though I could pass as a human, Mesula kept me locked away and trained me in the skills of the Vilsestra. I was taught cunning, survival and stealth. Above all, I was taught to use my powers over the winds, waters and skies – I was taught to control birds and to fly like them.'

'Cool,' breathed Izzie but Layah shushed her.

'I grew up in the shadows,' explained Mum. 'Mesula lived in fear that the villagers would find me and destroy me. She convinced the villagers that a deadly stranger haunted the Lowesdale Giant – this rumour soon grew and it poisoned the villagers with enough fear to keep them from the mountain and the forest.'

'So she – *both* of you – were the Lowesdale Stranger?' said Izzie, awed.

'James told me that the villagers discovered a hideout in the forest,' said Layah, 'built into the mountain. So that was where you lived?'

Her mum nodded. 'The rumours in the village kept us safe for a long time but some humans were braver than Mesula thought – people like Frank and Janet Bellford. They were amateur birdwatchers from Newbeck. Their daughter went to Lowesdale School and the three of them often went on long walks up the Lowesdale Giant, following birds deeper and deeper into the forest. Their daughter was Lauren Bellford.' She wasn't looking at them now; her face was darker and her voice bitter. 'One evening the Bellfords spotted me in the forest. It was just for a moment – a flash between the trees – but Mesula was scared. She was convinced that they would tell others and they would return with guns and dogs and hunt us out. I was older by then . . . by Vilsestra standards I had reached adulthood and Mesula decided to test me. She ordered me to kill the Bellford family. The thought disgusted me. Not only had Mesula underestimated human bravery, she had underestimated their kindness. Food parcels kept appearing in the forest, labelled 'for the stranger on the mountain'. Someone in the village had taken pity on the Lowesdale Stranger. This kindness taught me to hope in the goodness of humans. The little I'd seen of the villagers and farmers had shown me that they were – for the most part – peaceful. But Mesula was adamant that they would harm us and killing the Bellfords was the only way to keep our secret. She had tracked the Bellfords to their sweetshop in Newbeck, where they lived in the flat above.'

Layah felt the weight of the sugar mouse still in her pocket.

'But I had a plan,' continued Mum, 'a plan to save the Bellfords. On the night of my attack, Mesula and I travelled to Newbeck. She watched from the mountains and I went to the treetops near the village. I was to use my powers to create a storm and conjure a rod of lightning to strike the sweetshop and cause a fire. But as my storm raged, I directed the lightning – not to the sweetshop – but to a tree on the pavement outside. I thought that if the fire started in the tree that would give the Bellfords enough time to escape. I would be punished for my failure, but it was a risk I was willing to take.' She went on, 'As lightning struck the tree, I flew down into the village – but when I got closer, I saw that another storm, stronger than mine, was forcing the flaming branches towards the shop. Mesula had conjured her own storm from the clifftops and by the time I reached the shop, the fire had already caught hold. The howling of the wind and the hammering of the rain overpowered the sound of the fire – no one knew to raise the alarm and the street was deserted. All Vilsestra pride forgotten, I spread my wings and flew to the window – I saw them. Lauren and her parents were trapped in the corner, at the mercy of the flames. I called to them and was about to climb inside – to help them! To fly them to safety! – but suddenly there was an explosion and I was blasted off into the night.'

The bedroom was still and silent. Layah's chest was constricting. Even the clock seemed to have stopped ticking.

'The fire was unstoppable,' said Mum. 'No one could save them. I woke hours later, safe in the woods near Newbeck. I rushed back to the sweetshop and saw the damage – the building was burnt black – and Mesula was waiting for me.'

The girl's face was empty. She looked around at the skeleton of the room, once a home and now rubble.

'I understand now,' said the girl, 'I will always be stronger than the humans. The power I have . . . it will always set me apart. We are invincible, but we must always be invisible.'

'We are superior!' purred the Other. 'They are useless beings.'

'Then I know what I have to do.'

The girl held out the gold bracelet she had found on the forest floor. The Other began to laugh, a harsh mocking cackle which rose with the dirty smoke. The girl stood and waited.

'What childishness is this?' cawed the Other.

The girl gazed back at her, holding the bracelet steady.

'Mesula, I know the stories,' said the girl. 'I have read the Teachings about objects which can hold power. You told me the night I found the bracelet.'

'You foolish girl! Transferring a Vilsestra's power to an object is a punishment – remember the story of Mandalina – have you not been attending to your lessons?' Mesula snarled. 'The force alone could break you!'

'I'm willing to take that risk.'

Mesula stalked across the smoke-stained room and seized a handful of the girl's hair, dragging her closer.

'You would give up our Vilsestra ways? After everything I have done for you? Think of what we can achieve together – you are stronger than you know! Together we could reclaim this land – flood the streets, the houses, drown the humans in their beds – we can purge their cities, bring back true wilderness to the Lakes! Continue the Vilsestra legacy with pride!'

'No!' the girl screamed – a thunderclap shook the building – 'the Vilsestra legacy is history and dust! I will not bring a war on innocent people! I will not punish them for simply being different to us!'

With a screech, Mesula hurled the girl across the room and she crumpled into a corner. The girl rolled over, her lip bloody, her eyes blazing yellow, and she began to crawl back across the grimy floorboards. She snatched up the bracelet and held it up.

'If this is how you want to use my powers, to turn me into a murderer,' she choked, 'then I will no longer be a Vilsestra.'

The storm clouds broke and the rain came down like needles.

'You're not brave enough!' spat Mesula. 'A weakling is of no use to me!' A streak of lightning illuminated her haggard face. 'So do it! Invoke the ancient lore. Summon your final storm.'

The girl staggered to her feet, holding the bracelet before her. She began to recite in a peculiar, hoarse tongue:

'Take this object here

Trap my cracking soul

Cut all power bare

Never more be whole.'

The lightning, the thunder, the thudding in the girl's head was explosive – she couldn't see or think or stand. She was being pounded through darkness, spinning in timelessness. She saw a flash of yellow, a shrill scream and then . . . nothing. She opened her eyes, her face pressed against the dirty floorboards. She rose, crooked and unsteady, and looked around. The dawn was rising. The flat was empty. Both Mesula and the bracelet were gone.

The girl was cold. She had never felt cold before. Until now.

Layah's mum looked at her daughters, her eyes skimming their faces as if she was sketching them in her mind. It was a look of such pure love that Layah's eyes began to prickle and she looked away.

'I took Lauren's name,' continued Mum. 'I found documents and money in the flat and I went to London. Mesula hid the bracelet in the Lakes. That's why I returned: to find my powers so I can face Mesula once and for all.'

'So your powers are in the bracelet?' said Layah. 'The bracelet which belonged to Lauren Bellford?'

'Just like the Vilsestra from Babcia's poem,' added Izzie. 'Her powers were hidden in a helmet!'

'Yes. Lauren lost it in the forest and I kept it. That's where I've been going these past few days; I have been searching for the bracelet on the mountains. Today I found it.' She paused. 'I put my powers inside it so I could be human, so I could escape and make a life, a family, so I could one day have you.'

She stopped talking and turned away, looking out at the star-spotted sky.

'What was your name before?' asked Izzie quietly. 'Before Lauren?'

'Rianda.' She smiled.

'We forgive you, Mum,' said Izzie. 'You tried to save

them. You didn't mean to . . .'

'Ren . . .' Their dad half rose from the floor then slumped back, sloshing hot chocolate over his knees.

Their mum looked to Layah, who was staring at her hands, her heart thumping. Layah raised her eyes to her mum's face. All this time their mum had kept this from them. She was another person entirely! Yet at the same time, her mum had never been more herself. And Layah understood. She understood the fear of the girl hidden in the forest and she knew why she had done it. In her mind, Layah saw the fire and the family and her throat burnt with unshed tears for the girl who had grown up to be her mum.

Slowly, Layah stepped towards her.

'You're our mum and nothing will ever change that,' Layah croaked. 'We're with you. Whatever you need us to do. We won't let Mesula beat us.'

Layah had thought they were searching for a lost family, but here, in this cramped cottage, was all the family she needed.

'Thank you.' Her mum's voice was grave. 'Now my powers have returned, I was able to communicate with Mesula by Reflection. I was trying to reason with her, but she will not rest. She says Vilsestra cannot hide from what they are. I sensed that she was not in

168

Lowesdale, but she will return. She has been biding her time. I was stupid to think a few locks and sealed windows would keep her away. I've decided . . . I need to face her and you three need to leave. Your dad can take you back to London tonight—'

'What? No way,' protested Layah.

'Mum, we want to stay with you!' cried Izzie.

'No.' Their mum's eyes flashed. 'I made a mistake bringing you here. I thought I could protect you, but I was wrong. I have to face Mesula alone. Only a Vilsestra can destroy a Vilsestra.'

'But we can help!' Layah began arguing.

'No!' Mum shouted. 'Mesula has already started using you to scare me. The attack by the lake, on the island, the dead birds – she's threatening me!'

'I think we should listen to your mum,' hastened Dad, rising from the bed, still clutching his empty mug.

'Layah,' Mum pleaded, 'I can't let her hurt you and Izzie!'

The blood was pounding in Layah's head as she glanced at Izzie, who was bundled up in the huge bed, her eyes darting questioningly to Layah. Izzie wouldn't leave unless Layah did too.

Layah looked back at her mum, her resolve ebbing.

'OK,' Layah conceded, 'fine. Let's go home.'

Then the roof caved in.

# Chapter Eighteen

Smoke and sawdust burnt Layah's throat as she was hurled backwards against the wardrobe; the plywood frame splintered beneath her. Above them part of the roof had been torn away by a whirlwind so fierce it felt like a torrent of water.

Layah's hair was flying about her face, slitting her eyes and mouth. Her parents were scrunched in the corner by the window, arms over their heads. A debris of plaster and nails swamped the bed, obliterating Izzie from view. Layah tried to push herself up but she was pinned to the floor by the force of the wind. She shouted but the wind snatched her voice away. All she could do was stare as the dark figure, revolving slowly, descended amongst the chaos.

The Vilsestra was a mass of black rags writhing like snakes around her, and her huge, purple-tipped black wings were open wide. The only solid parts of her were her hands and face: stone-grey, puckered skin like a gargoyle. Her neck was elongated, inhuman; worst of all were her yellow eyes, wide and lidless with darting pupils. Her white hair rippled over her shoulders as she came to hover above the floor, a smile distorting her face.

'Layah.' She spoke in a wild voice, scratchy and shrill. 'Layah and Izobel. The traitor's children.'

'Don't talk to them!'

Layah's mum had risen to her feet, fighting against the wind.

'You've come for me, Mesula! Don't touch my daughters!' Mum shouted; Layah saw L.B.'s bracelet glinting on her mum's wrist.

'It is not for you to set the rules,' barked Mesula; her wings flinched, sending a shock wave through the room.

Layah felt the force of it pulsate through her and cried out, the mangled wardrobe cutting into her back. Mesula rolled her head towards Layah and she raised a hand, unfurling yellow fingernails.

'Keep away from her!' Mum yelled.

Layah saw a funnel of air whip across Mesula, jerking her hand to her side. She turned angrily back to face Layah's mum.

'I'm never coming back,' bellowed Mum, staggering against the gale. 'Leave me and my family alone.'

'You can't escape who you really are, Rianda!' Mesula spat. 'Vilsestra don't belong in their world.'

'Then I will fight you,' stammered Mum. 'We can settle this in a fight. If I die, you leave them alone. Vilsestra's honour. It'll be my life for theirs.'

'Mum, no! You can't—' But Layah's words barely rose above the wind.

'Death seeks those arrogant enough to challenge it.' Mesula laughed. 'You were always a foolish girl, but I cannot deny the urge to test you. I'm curious to see what outcome this may bring,' she cawed, those terrible eyes glinting towards Layah again.

Layah's mum shook her head from side to side, as if loosening herself, and Layah saw long nails flexing at the ends of her fingers. Her mum's neck was lengthening. She rolled back her shoulders and wings burst out of them, feathers fluttering along them until they were full and glossy.

'Ren! No!' Dad pleaded from the floor. 'REN!'

'At last, Rianda,' Mesula cackled.

'Layah, keep down!' yelled Mum and she sprang at Mesula.

Layah didn't know who was winning. Both Vilsestra were writhing together, a mass of twisting limbs and beating wings, fingernails spinning like knives, black

172

feathers ripped out in handfuls and scattered on the floor. Mesula smashed their mum against the window again and again, the glass shattering into the garden below. Layah fought to get up but the strength of wind was unbeatable. With a yell her mum grabbed the front of Mesula's cloak and, propelled by a blast of air, they both crashed through the window and out into the night. The pressure in the room dropped and Layah could breathe normally again. She scrambled to her feet. The screams and snarls from the garden continued to rip into the sky. Layah fell towards the bed and started chucking debris aside.

'Izzie! Izzie!'

Her dad was at her side, dragging away bricks and wooden panels. The dust was clogging their throats as they dug deeper into the rubble until Layah touched something warm.

'She's here, Dad! Izzie!'

Layah shoved aside a smashed lamp, revealing Izzie's small face beneath it, smeared in dust. Her dad let out a faint cry, scooping up his youngest daughter and dragging her into the light. The three of them retreated, bent low, into the dark corridor.

Their dad laid Izzie carefully on the floor; she blinked blearily up at them.

'She's OK!' he gasped.

Layah gripped his arm. 'Iz, can you hear us?'

'I'm fine,' croaked Izzie. 'Where's Mum?'

'Dad, get her cleaned up,' ordered Layah, listening to the shrieks from the garden.

'Layah! Where are you going?' he cried; he was as white as Izzie.

'I've got to help Mum!' Layah shouted.

'Layah, don't leave me too!'

Layah tore her arm out of her dad's grip and bolted down the stairs. She skidded into the kitchen and leapt over the shattered glass from the back door. Fear sharpened her mind, throwing up mad ideas. She grabbed the washing line from the grass and sprinted around the corner of the cottage. A torrent of wind and hail smacked her across the face. The two Vilsestra were locked in battle, forcing each other this way and that, six feet from the ground, their wings beating powerfully.

Layah ran forward, tying a loop in the washing line and hurling it at Mesula; the washing line caught one of Mesula's flailing ankles and Layah felt the knot tighten around it. She pulled and Mesula jerked backwards, her leg held fast. Layah's mum rose up above Mesula, summoning a thunder cloud crackling with electricity.

'Layah! Watch out!' called Mum.

Layah dragged Mesula along like a monstrous balloon and tied the washing line to the frame of the gate, the other end still binding Mesula's ankle. Her mum pointed her fists towards Mesula and there was a crack of white-blue lightning. Mesula was suddenly luminous, caught in the sparks, screaming and howling.

Layah saw her mum holding back, fluttering a few metres away, her arms lowering, looking – for a moment – concerned. Then her face filled with shock and Layah realised that Mesula's screams were not panic but laughter. In a flash of rain, the lightning was extinguished. The washing line snapped like thread. Mesula turned and Layah's mum was blasted out of the sky by a torrent of rain.

Layah's heart was beating in her ears – hope draining from her. Mesula was too powerful. She beat her wings, causing another crash of wind to flatten the garden, throwing Layah into a flowerbed. She pushed herself up and tried to crawl towards her mum's body but she was too late. Mesula conjured a jet of wind so strong it lifted Mum's limp body off the ground and into Mesula's arms.

'Stop! No! Stop!' cried Layah desperately.

The Vilsestra turned her ugly face towards Layah.

'Only fools dare to fight Vilsestra!' she sneered. 'We are the mighty Bird Singers! All human souls are weak, Layah, weak and foolish.'

Mesula rose, the wind rushing around her, her rags flaring up in the current. And, with Layah's mum captured in her arms, the Vilsestra disappeared into the darkness in a whirl of feathers and a crash of thunder.

# Chapter Nineteen

Rook Cottage hunched black in the still night. The sky was devoid of birdsong. A bedcover plastered the hole in their mum's bedroom like a giant bandage. At the edge of the hole, where the window had previously existed, a corner of the bedcover came unstuck and two sets of feet dangled out of the gap. Layah dropped to the ground, followed closely by Izzie, and they jogged down the track towards the main road.

'Keep your eyes open,' warned Layah. 'We need to be ready to run. Mesula could be hanging about and she's still got those scary crows working for her.'

'And don't forget Mor Hemlock,' whispered Izzie. 'She was supposed to be working for the Lowesdale Stranger, remember.'

'I reckon we could take Mor Hemlock,' muttered Layah.

An hour had passed since Mesula's victory but Layah was still fizzing with adrenaline. She was trying to ignore the dark hopelessness clawing inside her – she wouldn't let it distract her.

The sisters hurried up the road, scanning the quiet night, but there were no creeping shadows lurking to catch them, just fresh air and miles of open sky. The star-map above them was brighter than Layah had ever seen it; it was like a page from one of Izzie's encyclopaedias on the solar system.

'You think she's taken her to Avery Island, don't you?' said Izzie. 'That's where we're going, isn't it?'

'Yeah, that was the idea.'

If Mesula's old home on the mountain had been discovered then Avery Island would provide the perfect hideout for the Vilsestra. It was wild and isolated. Plus there was the tunnel where Izzie had seen the crows . . . what if they had been guarding something? Like a dungeon trapped in the heart of the island.

'Do you think Dad will be OK?' asked Izzie.

'Sure.' Layah shrugged. 'You left him that note telling him we've gone to get Mum. There's nothing he can do to stop us now.'

Their dad had collapsed when Layah had told them what had happened in the garden. He'd lain on the sofa, wringing his hands and mumbling in Polish. He had a nasty cut on his leg from the collapsed ceiling.

The girls had bandaged him up with a pillowcase and fed him some toast, hot milk and painkillers and he had promptly fallen asleep from exhaustion. Layah knew there was no way their dad would have let them leave the cottage, if he'd been in any state to stop them.

Layah did feel sorry for him, but they had already wasted valuable time – their dad's injury and his panicking would only slow them down.

'And you're sure Mum was OK?' Izzie asked for the seventh time.

'She's alive,' said Layah firmly, 'and we're going to save her.'

They crested the hump in the road and saw the entrance to Westwood Manor ahead, the white house gleaming in the starlight. They crept along the sandy driveway.

'Layah, don't you think we should come up with a plan first?' whispered Izzie.

'There isn't time!' replied Layah. 'We can go through the garden, get down to the jetty, grab the Vellamo and shoot off to the island before the Westwoods wake up. This way—'

Floodlights burst into life, trapping them in a rectangle of light. The girls froze, arms shielding their faces, as the Manor door banged open and a figure strode towards them.

'Father? Layah! Izzie! What are you doing here?'

James was wrapped in a dressing gown.

'We need to borrow your boat,' said Izzie, before Layah could speak.

'What!?'

'Look. Can we just come in?' said Layah. 'Um – please,' she added quickly.

Her politeness seemed to add to his confusion. They followed him inside and as the door closed the lights outside went out. *They must be triggered by a sensor*, thought Layah, feeling stupid. Had she really believed they could just march into the Manor and hop on the Westwoods' speedboat?

James gestured to the library door, still rubbing his face. They trailed after him and saw a book and a mug of tea in a winged armchair.

'It's ten o'clock at night!' said James. 'You're in trouble, aren't you?'

'Where's your dad?' said Layah, glancing around the library as if Henry might be squatting on a shelf.

'He's out,' said James vaguely. 'So . . . what did you say about a boat?'

'We don't need any boats, that was a joke,' said Layah

180

quickly, nudging Izzie with her foot.

'It was a joke,' said Izzie, nodding manically.

'Look, James, we – wait! What are you wearing?' Layah took a step back to take in his parsley-coloured pyjamas dotted with little Ws.

'The Westwood family crest.' He blushed. 'And before you start judging, they're really comfy, OK!'

'Maybe now isn't the time to talk about pyjamas,' interjected Izzie.

'Look!' James picked up the book from the armchair. 'I got this from the Newbeck library and it's all about other creatures which turned out to be normal people. The Bloody Man from Dranmere was discovered to be a painter who'd slipped in a bucket of red paint. And the Wolf of Wagsnare turned out to be the old lady who ran the fancy dress shop – but it just proves—'

'It's real!' interrupted Layah. 'The Lowesdale Stranger – the rumours are true!'

'What?' Layah was surprised James's eyebrows didn't jump off his face in shock. 'What are you talking about?'

'Quiet!' cried Izzie.

The outdoor lights had flicked on and a car was crunching down the driveway. Flashing lights shimmered through the library's open door and they heard the slamming of car doors.

'The police! We can't let them find us!' swore Layah, grabbing Izzie's arm, ready to run.

'Over here.' James leapt into action. 'Quick!'

'We can't hide from the police!' squeaked Izzie.

'We've got to!' shot back Layah, as they heard the peal of the front doorbell. 'They are not going to stop us saving Mum!'

James sprinted across the library to a bookcase at the far end. In a swift movement he had unslotted a segment of shelves and was running his hands along the wall behind it. There was an impatient *knock-knock-knock* at the front door.

'Got it! Inside!' commanded James.

He had pushed open a door, which had laid flush with the wallpaper, revealing a staircase beyond.

'Wow! A secret staircase!' said Izzie.

'It leads up to my bedroom,' said James. 'It wasn't designed as a hideout, but it should do for now. Don't make any noise. I'll get rid of them.'

He pulled the door shut behind them and they heard him resealing the entrance with the bookcase. Layah looked round at Izzie, who had sat down on the first step, hugging her knees. Layah dropped down next to her.

'Do you think he knows what's going on?' whispered Izzie.

'What? James? No. I don't think "Their mum's been abducted by a giant bird-woman" is something he would have guessed.'

The stairwell was almost totally soundproof so there was no way of hearing what was going on in the rest of the house.

'I can't believe Dad called the police,' Layah sighed. 'Doesn't he realise he's putting Mum in danger?'

If the police found out about their mum, who knew what they'd do to her. They'd call her a freak, a monster – something to be caged, like a wild animal.

'But how did he find out we'd gone so quickly?' said Izzie. 'It doesn't make sense.'

There was a bang of a door being thrown open. Someone had entered the library. Layah and Izzie pressed their ears to the wall. It was like listening through water but Layah could make out footsteps and the knock and scrape of furniture being moved.

'Sorry it's a little untidy.' James's voice was surprisingly close to the secret stairwell. 'Usually, the police give me a bit of warning before they swing by. I get the chalk out – draw a couple of body outlines on the carpet!'

'I'd dispense with the wisecracks if I was you,' came a hard, Scottish female voice, also close by. 'Being a

183

Westwood doesn't make you untouchable. I've locked up plenty of your kind before.'

'Oh, I didn't realise I was the "wrong kind",' came James's voice, and Layah felt a rush of solidarity with him.

'What DCI Swift means is cut the lip, lad,' a male voice interjected.

'Thank you, DI Blackmore, I know what I meant!' said DCI Swift tartly. 'Let's search the bedrooms.'

The voices and footsteps became muffled. Layah gave Izzie an encouraging smile.

'As soon as they're gone, we go,' strategised Layah. 'If we can't get to the Vellamo, we should go down to the Boating Centre.'

'Layah, wait!' Izzie started. 'I don't think we can go to the island just yet.'

'Why? I know it's scary. I can go alone if—'

'No!' Izzie cried. 'I mean, we need to know more – we need to find out how to defeat Mesula.'

'We'll figure it out on the way,' improvised Layah frantically.

'I don't think we can just make it up. Mythical monsters are rarely easy to kill,' said Izzie seriously.

'And you know this from your long experience of killing mythical monsters!'

Despite her sarcasm, hopelessness was sapping Layah's energy. Here was another speedbump in their race to save their mum.

'If only Babcia was here, we could have called her,' Layah sighed. 'I bet she'd know what to do.'

'Babcia believed in asking questions – in doing your research. So I think we should go and see Mr Speckleback,' said Izzie, holding up the birdwatcher's calling card.

'Izzie, we can't trust him!' moaned Layah. 'He might tell the police.'

'But he was the one who told us about the shapeshifters. He actually believed us when we said the feathers came from a woman!'

There was a grinding noise and Izzie flinched in alarm. James appeared above them, looking grave.

'James, we need to borrow the Vellamo,' said Layah, pushing herself to her feet – there was no point tiptoeing around the issue, she decided.

'Woah! Not so fast!'

'Fine! Then we need to leave.' Layah glowered.

'Layah! The police are looking for you and your mum,' James interrupted. 'Apparently someone reported a disturbance at the cottage and now they think you're missing. I want to help you, but you need to tell me what's going on. What's all this about the Lowesdale Stranger?'

Izzie gave Layah an encouraging prod with her elbow.

'OK. I'll tell you,' sighed Layah exasperatedly, 'but it's going to sound totally mad!'

But she explained, as best she could, everything that had happened since he'd scooted her back to Rook Cottage. Even as Layah spoke she couldn't quite comprehend the memory full-on, seeing it in snippets: the snarl of the lightning, her mum's cry, and Mesula's yellow eyes taunting Layah as she carried her mum away. She left out the story of L. Bellford and the fire; that part seemed too private to share.

When she had finished, there was a long pause as James looked from sister to sister.

'Is this some kind of joke?' he said slowly.

'We're not lying!' stressed Layah.

It stung that James didn't believe her – even though it wasn't surprising. Layah didn't think she'd have believed it herself.

'Layah's telling the truth. We've even got evidence,' said Izzie stoutly, handing the box of Vilsestra feathers to James. 'Remember these?'

James, his face slack with shock, turned the box over in his hands.

'You told me you didn't see any footprints by the lake,' said Layah. 'That's because Mesula can fly – that's how she got away so quickly.'

'What about the note I got?' asked James. 'Telling me to go to the lake.'

'I dunno. Why is that important?' Layah had almost forgotten about the note.

'Maybe it was from Mr Speckleback?' interrupted Izzie.

'It doesn't matter,' said Layah, 'we need to get going!'

'Hold up!' said James, raising a hand. 'You're going to go charging after this bird-lady-thing—'

'Mesula,' interjected Izzie patiently, 'the Vilsestra.'

'You're going to go charging after this Mesula, the Vilsestra, when she's already proven herself to be powerful. It's too dangerous!'

Layah was losing patience. She wasn't going to let James stand in their way.

'Duh! Mesula is powerful and this *is* dangerous!' yelled Layah. 'Aren't you listening? That's why we need to get to Avery Island as soon as possible! She's got our mum!'

Layah glowered at James but Izzie stepped between them. She squeezed Layah's arm and gave her a bright trust-me smile before turning to James.

'James. Please. We've got a plan,' said Izzie soothingly. 'First we need to visit Teddington Speckleback's emporium and we need *you* to get us into the village without being seen. And we need to go right now!'

# Chapter Twenty

Layah wasn't sure whether James fully believed their story, but he had agreed to drive them into the village (avoiding Izzie's request to see his driving licence). Layah had reluctantly admitted that driving with a fourteen-year-old driver was the least of their worries right now. It wasn't exactly what you'd call 'travelling in style', thought Layah, as she lay nose-down on the floor of the silver Jaguar. But if the police were looking for them, they needed to be careful. They couldn't afford any more delays; the detour to Mr Speckleback was bad enough. There was still no sign of Henry and it made Layah feel on edge. James hadn't said when he was due back and Layah didn't think Henry would be happy if he found them using his house as a hideout.

A thick silence lay over the sleeping village as the car whined through the empty streets. Teddington Speckleback's emporium was on the far side of

Lowesdale, down a flight of stone steps and along a cobbled alleyway between two houses. It was marked by a peeling sign over an arched doorway.

Izzie knocked smartly on the emporium door but there was no response.

The alleyway was murky and there was an odd scratching coming from a dark corner. Layah felt twitchy. She was about to say they should return to the car – the birdwatcher was clearly asleep – when there was a low call from within. The door clicked and Izzie opened it, revealing a velvet curtain; she pushed it aside and Layah followed her.

It was the strangest place Layah had ever been: dark and cramped, the four walls were covered with framed feathers dotted with labels; the frames were stacked higgledy-piggledy on top of each other. There were feathers in jars, crammed on two big dusty desks, and more feathers hanging from the ceiling like bunches of herbs. A couple of stuffed birds glared with painted eyes, trapped in glass cabinets.

Layah gazed through the murky darkness.

'Where d'you reckon he is?' she breathed to Izzie, anxiety growing in the pit of her stomach.

Before Izzie could answer there was a squeaky cough and Mr Speckleback emerged from a corner, as birdlike as ever and clad in a chequered dressing gown.

'Given your teachers the slip, eh?' he trilled.

'We came to ask for your help,' said Izzie.

'Help!' he spluttered. 'What help can a simple birdwatcher offer?'

'Mr Speckleback, we think the feathers we showed you are from a Vilsestra,' said Izzie slowly. 'Well, we know they are . . .'

'You know? Proof! Proof must come before knowing,' Mr Speckleback twittered excitedly.

'We have proof,' explained Izzie softly, 'we've seen her. We've seen two of them. Do you know what they are?'

'Goodness me, yes! Yes, of course. I know the myth of the Vilsestra well,' he babbled, 'but *two* Vilsestra! Full studies of the species must be made. We will need the proper equipment for this inspection!'

He started burrowing through his desk drawers, pulling out binoculars, sketchbook, pens and, with a tinkle of steel, a handful of small knives.

An image of the dead bird in the hedgerow burst in to Layah's mind.

'No! What are you doing?' Layah cried. 'No one is getting dissected here! We just need to know how to destroy one.'

'Destroy without study?' whimpered Mr Speckleback,

nervously dropping a magnifying glass. 'And two Vilsestra to destroy? You girls must be getting extra credit for this! Homework truly has got more hands-on these days . . .'

'Not two. We just want to destroy one,' said Layah. 'The other one is . . . we don't want any harm to come to her. Do you know what we need to do or not?'

Mr Speckleback glared at her; the vein in his temple twitched.

'I am sorry, my excitement has distracted me somewhat,' he panted. 'It's not every day one has proof of an ancient ornithological creature living nearby. For protection from evil, I would have suggested the Greek *mátia* or the Polish amber, but I see you already have the amber.'

He nodded to their necklaces.

'But to destroy! Actively, deliberately, end,' continued Mr Speckleback. 'I shall need my books.'

He stumbled away into a corner and returned holding a battered red volume. Izzie gave a little 'aw' noise as if Mr Speckleback had just produced an adorable kitten. He held it up and Layah noticed the name:

'A. Kosmatka!' she cried. 'Hey! That's our babcia. What's that book?'

'*Myths and Monsters: A Study of Creatures from*

*European Storytelling* by Professor Ana Kosmatka,' supplied Mr Speckleback, 'a remarkable lady. Little did she know that her studies would be of use in our modern world today.' He flicked through the pages. 'Ah hah! Vilsestra. You' – he flapped the book at Izzie – 'read aloud.'

Izzie took the book and, with a nervous glance at Layah, she read: '*Vilsestra. There are many monstrous females in ancient poems; however, after many years of study, it is my belief that several of these creatures, heavily associated with birds, may all be described under the name "Vilsestra". The Vilsestra are powerful beasts: women warriors, descended from goddesses, with the wings of birds and strength of storms. In some tales, they are described as monstrous bloodthirsty fiends, yet in others they are beautiful sorceresses who charm the skies and punish evil with great tempests. Vilsestra are not immortal but their great powers make them near impossible to vanquish. Only the poem "King Vukasin and Mandalina" gives the reader any clue of how a Vilsestra might be destroyed.* And then it's the poem,' said Izzie, holding up the book.

Layah sank against a table. The poem held the clue to destroying a Vilsestra.

Layah could almost see Babcia peering over her

purple spectacles, coaxing in her calm voice: 'Each word has many meanings; it is a difficult job picking the right one. No word or sentence is there by mistake.'

Layah blinked away the memory. She looked over at Izzie.

'OK, Iz, how do we work out the clue from the poem?' said Layah. 'King Vukasin sees Mandalina asleep, and he steals her helmet so he can control her and she can fight his battles.'

'Her *spell-bound helmet*,' recited Izzie. 'We know Vilsestra can put their power into an object. The poet got that part right.'

'Could we do that to Mesula?' said Layah uncertainly.

Izzie was studying the poem again. 'I don't know. But Vukasin doesn't use the helmet to kill her; he uses her bow.'

'He snatches it.' Layah nodded. 'But why didn't Mandalina just electrocute him? How come she gets killed by a bow and arrow? You'd think she'd be more powerful than that.'

'Look.' Izzie pointed. 'I think this is the important line here: *Only weapon took from her heathen grasp / Could have smote that creature's life to dust.* Only a weapon taken from a Vilsestra – a Vilsestra-made weapon – can destroy a Vilsestra.'

'So we've got to find a Vilsestra weapon?' said Layah, exasperated. 'How are we supposed to do that?'

'Oh! How silly of me! I forgot.' Mr Speckleback let out a twittering giggle.

He twirled about and disappeared. He fluttered back a moment later with a dark case, the kind used for a musical instrument. He inserted a copper key into the lock. The joints creaked as he opened the lid and Layah and Izzie moved closer.

Nestled in faded silk was a black-wood crossbow. Three arrows, tipped with purple-black feathers, slotted into the lid. It looked like something from a museum.

'Is this the real crossbow from the poem?' said Layah warily.

'It is claimed to be a Vilsestra crossbow, yet not necessarily the same as Mandalina's.' Mr Speckleback sniffed, as if that were was obvious.

'But does it still work? It looks kind of old,' said Layah doubtfully.

'Work?' he squeaked. 'It's got all its parts so I'd say it works! Beautiful specimen. A recent donation from a university in Krakow. Such a beauty.'

He ran a light finger over the box.

'Layah! I think this could work!' said Izzie excitedly. 'It's a loophole. Only a Vilsestra can kill a Vilsestra, that's what Mum—'

'Iz!' Layah cut across her but Mr Speckleback's eyes had already widened.

'Study of any Vilsestra or their offspring,' said Mr Speckleback slowly, 'would be most fascinating, not to mention richly . . . profitable for the enhancement of ornithological knowledge.'

Layah didn't like the way he was looking at Izzie. His twittering manner had been replaced by that sinister stillness.

'So can we – um – borrow this? Or we can pay,' said Layah, before she remembered she didn't have any money, 'but we might have to come back later . . .'

Mr Speckleback closed the case with a snap.

'No payment. No payment,' he rambled, flustered again. 'I am a man of learning. You can take it.'

'Thank you!' Izzie beamed.

She made to take it, but Mr Speckleback held on, his eyes fixed on her face.

'I wish to meet one of them,' he said, 'to study. That's all I care about. To study a Vilsestra. Dead or alive. Whichever one dies,' he added lightly.

Layah stared disgustedly at the little man.

'When we succeed in destroying her, we'll let you know where we leave the body,' said Layah coldly.

The old man released the case into Izzie's arms. He gave Layah a cracked smile.

'Iz, we should go,' Layah muttered.

Mr Speckleback's eyes darted after them as they picked their way across the room and out into the night. The alleyway was somehow darker than before. The walls of the houses on either side seemed to be leaning in, seeping them in shadow. Layah squinted towards the road; she could just make out the car and James's silhouette at the wheel.

'Come on,' whispered Layah but before they had moved two steps they heard something. Her blood froze.

*Tap-tap, tap-tap.*

The sound of the cane echoed down the alleyway, bouncing off the walls.

'Go!' shouted Layah.

And the two of them, Izzie still clutching the case with the crossbow, broke into a run. The open street was only a few steps ahead of them—

Mor Hemlock burst from the shadows, like a moth from a cupboard, blocking their escape – brandishing her cane like a poker, she bore down upon them.

'Stop!' Her voice was like cold frost. 'You should not be here!'

Layah reacted instinctively – she ducked and swerved to avoid the flailing cane but Mor Hemlock had lunged at Izzie. They struggled, then Izzie tore the case free and Mor Hemlock was left holding a buckle from her coat sleeve. The two sisters pelted across the road and bowled into the car.

James was ready and the car's wheels skidded on to the road. Layah reached over and slammed the car door shut as they picked up speed.

Mor Hemlock was left in the dust, her white eyes flickering, Izzie's coat buckle dangling in her hand.

# CHAPTER TWENTY-ONE

The blue mountains surrounding Lowesdale stood quiet as ever-present ghosts. Layah looked out of James's bedroom window over the damp lawn and the smooth lake below. The Vellamo speedboat rocked in the water and the *Jiya* Wayfarer lay like a giant white shell on the grass.

It was nearly midnight and it was time to rescue their mum.

The moon was bright and Layah didn't know if this was a comfort or not. It would certainly help their progress across the lake, but James had told them about the police patrol boat. The visibility would make them a clear target.

'You ready for this?' said Layah.

'I think so,' replied Izzie, who was crouched on the carpet, rummaging through a crate. 'I just hope Mum's OK.'

Layah couldn't answer. She knew that if she let her

mind dwell on what was happening to her mum, even for a second, she'd be overcome with despair. Layah knew what Babcia would have said: 'Deal with each challenge piece by piece.' Just thinking about Babcia made Layah smile. She felt stronger.

After their encounter with Mor Hemlock they couldn't afford to waste any more time. Layah was convinced that she had been sent as a lookout by Mesula – now Mesula knew the sisters had teamed up with James, she may already be planning an attack on the Manor. They had to act now.

On their return to the Manor, the three of them had raided the Westwoods' store cupboards, looking for anything which might help them. Their spoils had been placed in the crate Izzie was now sorting: a length of boating rope, two head torches, a cigarette lighter, a tennis racket, a bottle of petrol, an old T-shirt and a packet of ginger biscuits (for emergencies only). Layah had tested out the crossbow in the Westwoods' library. Izzie had found a book on medieval weaponry and she read out instructions while Layah wrestled with the crossbow. At last she managed to fire an arrow across the room – impaling an unfortunate pineapple, which they'd balanced on top of a pile of books. Layah was pleased but they didn't have time for more than a ten-minute practice.

A ticking clock had started in Layah's brain. It had been over two hours since their mum had been captured. Layah looked at her sister; they were each wearing one of James's faded black hoodies – an attempt at camouflage.

'I think we've got everything,' said Izzie.

'Good.' Layah nodded. 'Then let's go and save Mum.'

Carrying the crate between them, they went out into the corridor. Layah was about to descend the stairs when a memory made her pause.

'Iz, I need to check something, come on.'

They placed the crate on the floor, glancing down the stairwell; James must still be in the library, cleaning up the mess they'd made during crossbow practice. Izzie behind her, Layah retraced her steps from the day before and slipped into Henry's office.

The room looked just as spotless as it had the first time.

'This is where Mum decided not to come on the picnic,' explained Layah, 'and I was thinking . . . she told us it was only yesterday that she finally found the bracelet, so I thought—'

'She found the bracelet here?' exclaimed Izzie. 'But how?'

'The painting!' cried Layah, dashing to it.

The sky-blue painting with the golden hoops had turned navy in the dim light. It looked rather like a pasta painting Layah had done when she was five.

'I knew it! The hoop things are stuck on,' said Layah. 'Bet they're real gold!'

'Layah, look here, there's a gap! One of the hoops is missing.'

Izzie ran her fingers over a dry, circular mark near the bottom of the painting.

'But why would Mum's bracelet . . . why would her hidden Vilsestra power be here in the Westwoods' manor?' mused Layah. 'Yesterday James he said he was looking for his Vespa keys in here but . . . was that the truth?'

Layah suddenly felt sick with embarrassment and stupidity. Had James been lying to them all this time? He'd rushed out of the room the second her mum had arrived – Layah had assumed he'd felt awkward after she'd refused to go to the library with him – but was it possible that he had been afraid of Layah's mum?

'We should get to the Vellamo,' whispered Layah, feeling a chill creeping over her. 'We ditch James, if we can. I should have known he was a lying son of a—'

'*Ogórki*!' Izzie shrieked like a siren.

Layah spun around to see James standing in the doorway to the bedroom. He was holding a small silver case.

'Having a last-minute pep talk without me?' He grinned fleetingly, but his eyes darted between them.

'What's that?' Layah nodded at the case.

'Ah! One final thing which I think might be more useful than those ginger biscuits.' He was fiddling with the lid, pressing in a code. 'My dad keeps a handgun in here.'

The lid clicked and James thrust it open to reveal . . . nothing. The case was empty.

'Well, that wasn't what I was expecting,' said James slowly. 'You don't think Mesula took it? She could have broken in when we left for the emporium!'

'I don't think guns are her style,' muttered Layah.

'Well, where is it, then?'

'Maybe your dad hid it in the library?' said Izzie sweetly. 'Maybe you should look in there?'

'Oh yes! Brilliant idea.' Layah nodded, cottoning on. 'You go to the library and we'll go down to the boat.'

James's eyes widened suspiciously.

'Well, maybe, but . . .' He frowned. 'No, we should go. I doubt Father would have misplaced the gun; if it's not here, it's not anywhere.' He placed the empty case on the bed. 'I thought you wanted to get going?'

Layah gritted her teeth, but there was no point arguing – they didn't want him to know what they'd found out. They needed James; the question was, what did he need from them?

James had been so keen to unmask the Lowesdale Stranger as a fake . . . Layah reminded herself. Would he keep their secret? What if James thought the Vilsestra were something to be studied in a museum or a zoo? Just like Mr Speckleback. What if he'd been planning this all along . . .

'Come on, you two!' James called from the corridor. 'Or I'll be enjoying a moonlit tour of the lake alone!'

Izzie and Layah glanced at each other and came to a silent agreement. There wasn't time to think of another plan.

But Layah wasn't taking any chances. James Westwood could no longer be trusted.

# CHAPTER TWENTY-TWO

Ren's eyes shot open. A high ceiling of dirt domed above her. She was tied to a stone slab, cords tight on her wrists and ankles. The whistling which had awoken her died away.

Mesula was standing in the shadows, L.B.'s bracelet glittering in her hand.

'This network is deep,' said the Vilsestra, opening her arms to the chamber. 'Water was my tool for digging it. It is an amazingly strong resource of ours. The strength of a lake.'

'Where are my daughters?' cried Ren, her voice waking with a croak. 'If you've hurt them, I swear I'll—'

A snap cut the air as Ren pulled her hand from its bond. She yelled with triumph but Mesula dived at her, gripping her wrist and forcing it back against the rock.

'Your children are not damaged.' Mesula leered. 'Not yet.'

'You've won. You've got me,' Ren panted, 'so kill

me. Punish me, but leave my family alone.'

'Kill you?' Mesula glared down at her. 'Why would I kill one of my own kind when there are so few of us left? I am keeping the Teachings of the Vilsestra alive!'

Ren dropped back on to the stone, her chest convulsing.

'That is all you've ever cared about!' gasped Ren. 'Your obsession with the old ways. Killing the Bellfords was never a show of strength – it was an act of fear. You wanted to turn me into a monster, just like you.'

'They threatened us!' Mesula screamed, her face a mask of anger. 'Do you not understand the damning greed of humans? They steal our ancient treasures, they burn wilderness and unmask mystery. I could not risk them taking you from me!'

Mesula's words vibrated in the air and Ren gazed up at her.

'I sacrificed my powers to be human.' Ren spoke slowly. 'So let me be human. Destroy the bracelet, if that's what you want. I'll never use my Vilsestra powers again. I just want my family safe.'

Mesula pulled the cord tight on Ren's wrist and secured it to the rock. She gave a dry laugh.

'You think that little sacrifice you made when you were a child can protect your human nest?' She sniffed.

'Your daughters are outside of your protection.'

Mesula paused and a smile curled her lips.

'Remind me, Rianda,' she hissed. 'Layah has a birthday coming up, does she not? Thirteen years old.'

Ren snarled and surged upwards again but Mesula slammed her back down.

'No! I know what you want to do – you can't!' roared Ren. 'I won't let you!'

'Oh, save the melodrama for later,' said Mesula. 'I'm sure your dear daughters will join in with the hysterics once they arrive.'

Ren's struggling renewed but Mesula was losing interest. 'Your daughters won't be long now,' Mesula sighed, 'my accomplice has informed me. I am looking forward to getting to know them better – your Layah and little Izobel.'

Ren screamed curses at Mesula but the old Vilsestra did not flinch as she tightened the knots with slow and steady hands.

# CHAPTER TWENTY-THREE

Layah watched James's profile as he steered the Vellamo across the dark lake. They hadn't spoken much since setting off, but James seemed sombre. He could be thinking of their daunting task ahead, but Layah wasn't so sure. They couldn't trust him.

She touched her amber pendant. She doubted the necklaces were actually going to be useful during a fight but it still gave her a warming comfort. It felt like Babcia was urging them onwards.

It was the deepest hour of the night and, as the Vellamo purred through the water, it would have been easy to believe they were the only people for miles. Far across the lake, the village was muffled in velvety darkness. The mountains looked as if they were carved from black clouds, their highest peaks enchanted by grey mist. Even at night, there was no denying the wonderous beauty of it all.

Izzie moved closer to Layah on the bench. 'Layah, I

need to say something important.'

Layah glanced over at James, who was staring straight ahead. The chug of the engine was loud but was it loud enough to cover their voices?

'What's up?' Layah whispered.

'I was thinking about what Mr Speckleback said.'

'What about?'

'About studying the Vilsestra and their offspring.'

'*Offspring*. Man! He makes Mum sound like an animal,' said Layah bitterly, 'like she's just some species to be collected to that old freak.'

'No, Layah. I think when he said "offspring" he meant us,' continued Izzie. 'All parents pass something to their children. A bit of both of them.'

'Yeah, and I've got Dad's rectangular toes,' grumbled Layah. 'Thanks, Dad . . .'

'Yes, but I was thinking about what we've got from Mum,' said Izzie, her eyes shining. 'From the Vilsestra part of Mum, I mean.'

Layah gazed back at her sister; there was a look of beaming excitement on Izzie's face.

'What? Like . . . her powers?' said Layah, frowning.

'You remember when the birds were chasing us,' said Izzie breathlessly, 'and Dad couldn't get the boat to start but then there was that wave, which pushed us to safety?'

'Yes . . . but that was just the engine, wasn't it?' said Layah.

'At the moment the wave appeared,' Izzie rushed on, 'I slammed my hands on to the side of the boat and it was kind of like – like I'd created the wave. I felt this strange sort of whooshing inside me – it whooshed right through me and suddenly the wave burst out of the water.'

'I've never felt anything like that,' muttered Layah, her heart sinking.

'I don't know – maybe I imagined it,' backtracked Izzie quickly. 'I mean, we'd know if we had *powers*! Wouldn't we?'

Layah looked out over the lake. She had never felt anything like Izzie described – the theory seemed like wishful thinking on Izzie's part. It was a nice idea but in reality all they had was courage, determination and luck – and they were going to need it. Layah's heart quickened.

'We might not have powers,' said Layah, 'but we're not letting Mesula win without a fight!'

Babcia's amber necklace felt strangely warm against her chest. Layah looked up to see James's head flick back to face the front. He'd been listening.

The Vellamo slid beside the jetty on Avery Island and

Izzie jumped out to tie the rope to the mooring pole. Layah scrambled up beside her and they both turned to look up at the island.

The island looked different at night. Layah had not noticed the denseness of the forest before, which curled around the hilltop. There was just a whisper of wind here, so distant it was almost like a voice; like the whistling which had woken Layah in Rook Cottage. She couldn't say for certain that it wasn't the same sound.

Layah glanced out at the lake; something had caught her eye – a flash of movement. She scanned the navy waters, unable to see anything.

'We should get moving before the police find us,' said Layah. 'Hand me that rope. We can't carry the crossbow in that violin case.'

Izzie opened the case and Layah managed to attach the crossbow to her back with the boating rope. Izzie had the ingenious idea of adding a walking sock, which they'd found in the boat, to Layah's belt to hold the three Vilsestra-feathered arrows.

'Right,' said Layah, 'I think we should head to the tunnel where Izzie saw the birds. Iz, you show us the way.'

Izzie nodded and marched forward like a tourist guide. They moved silently through the trees, tracing the tideline of the island in a circular direction. The low hum of the wind followed them. Layah glanced around, forcing her breath out slowly, trying to quieten the furious rhythm of her heart. The trees were empty of animal life. Not even a squirrel moved in the darkness. Their absence was eerily unnatural.

'It was down there,' whispered Izzie as the woodland path bent in an almost sheer descent. 'I fell the first time I found it.'

Their feet twisted sideways as they half-crawled down the slope towards the blot in the hillside that was the tunnel mouth. Layah's feet slipped and she caught at knots of grass to keep her balance. When they reached the tunnel, the ground levelled out so they could stand at its entrance. Layah turned to the others.

'Do you want to sort out the racket now?' said Layah stiffly to James.

James held out the tennis racket he'd been carrying under his arm. The old T-shirt, soaked in petrol, had been wound around the racket's head.

'One of my old favourites,' sighed James, trying to tempt a smile from Layah. 'He's seen me through many a match, has good old Tenny here.'

'Stop messing and light it up,' said Layah, handing James the lighter.

James put the flame to the racket, which burst with fire at once.

'I said this caveman's torch would work!' said James proudly.

'That ought to deal with those crows.' Layah nodded. 'Izzie and I have the headtorches too. Now I'll take the racket. James, you stay here and—'

'No. This isn't what we agreed. I'm coming with you.' James took a step towards her.

'We agreed you'd take us to the island,' retorted Layah, 'and you have, so thank you and goodbye.'

'Layah, you know I can help! I'm useless waiting up here.'

'You think we can't handle this?' snarled Layah.

'No. I didn't mean that!' James ran a hand through his hair. 'I'm sure you could handle anything on your own – you're so brave and, well, a little on the stubborn side which means you'd never give up. You're more of a hero than I could ever be. But I just want to help. Three is better than two.'

Layah scowled at him.

'Layah, let him come,' said Izzie, giving her a knowing look. 'He can go ahead.'

'OK! Fine!' grumbled Layah. 'We need to get moving. James, you take the racket. Go on, then.'

James walked forward into the tunnel and started down into the blackness. He had to bend slightly, his hair brushing dirt from the roof, his footsteps hollow and cautious.

The sisters looked at each other.

'We mustn't let him know we suspect him,' whispered Izzie. 'We still don't know if he's up to anything.'

'We need to stay alert,' muttered Layah. 'This is about you and me and Mum!'

Izzie nodded firmly. Layah looked down the tunnel, the lit racket sparking in her eyes.

'No turning back now,' said Layah, setting her teeth. 'Let's do it.'

'For Mum.' Izzie nodded. 'And for Dad.'

So they bent down and entered the tunnel, down into the veins of the island after James. Layah's fingers gripped an arrow on her belt, watching the back of James's head. How far was she willing to go to protect her family? She supposed she was about to find out.

# Chapter Twenty-Four

Their progress through the tunnel was slow. James was having trouble navigating the flaming racket, whilst avoiding the sharp rocks in the ceiling. Layah and Izzie lurched after him, the beams of their head torches flitting in the darkness.

Layah kept glancing behind them; the circle of moonlight at the tunnel entrance slowly receded to the size of a coin then disappeared completely. Their path was dipping downwards, deeper and deeper. Layah wondered if they would end up under the lake.

'Stop,' gasped Izzie, 'I thought I heard something.'

'What's wrong?' Layah asked, stumbling to a standstill.

'I thought I heard a rumbling,' said Izzie, smoothing the wall with her hands, 'coming from the wall. Do you think this tunnel is properly secure?'

There was a wobble in Izzie's voice and Layah

glanced up nervously at the dark ceiling. It was dense and heavy.

'I don't hear anything,' said James, raising the racket.

Layah placed her hand next to her sister's. She was about to tell Izzie it was nothing, but then – Layah took a sharp intake of breath. She could feel it too. Gentle rhythmic vibrations were coming from the tunnel wall. Layah looked up. Fragments of dirt shook from the ceiling and dust tickled Layah's cheek. The air seemed to grow heavy, thumping in Layah's ears.

'Something's in the tunnel,' Izzie gasped.

'We've got to keep moving,' commanded Layah, 'come on. Quick.'

Crouched and sweaty, they stumbled forward, breaking into an unsteady jog. Layah could hear something now. A whirring noise growing louder and louder. As they turned a bend, Layah looked back. The light of her headtorch would only go so far but she saw them, swift as speeding darts. The crows were chasing them.

'Run faster!' screamed Layah and they hurtled down the black tunnel.

Izzie tripped but Layah caught her. The tunnel was visibly humming with the sound of wings, the ceiling shook and dirt and pebbles showered them. Layah saw James slowing.

'What are you doing?' cried Layah, zipping past him.

'This should slow them down!' he shouted back.

Pulling a bottle of petrol from his pocket, he tipped it into the path then threw down the flaming racket. The petrol caught fire at once, the flames rushing up the walls, forming a hoop of fire between them and the charging crows.

'Keep going!' Layah shouted, shoving James ahead of her.

They bolted around another bend and there was a crunch – Layah looked up to see a jagged crack tearing through the roof. Before she could scream a warning, there was an explosion and Layah saw James hurl Izzie out of the way, diving after her. Layah tried to follow but she was too late; a deluge of plummeting rocks forced her backwards. She tried to call to Izzie but soil blocked her throat and she choked.

As the dust cleared, Layah saw an avalanche of dirt jamming the passageway, blocking Izzie and James from view. There was a cawing scream; Layah's headtorch flashed behind her and she saw the darting shadows of feathers and flames back along the tunnel. The crows had reached the circle of fire.

'Izzie! Are you OK? *Izzie!*' Layah cried, pushing

desperately against the rubble.

There was no sound from beyond it, but behind her, Layah heard a renewed rush of wings. The fire clearly hadn't made much difference to the crows and they were growing closer with each thud of her pounding heart.

A second explosion forced Layah backwards on to the ground. The mound of earth had burst open as if a cannonball had shot through it, firing at the approaching crows. A gale-force wind pressed the birds back and they bounced and flattened against the walls of the tunnel, writhing and shrieking.

Layah raised her head to see Izzie, her arms outstretched, directing the funnel of air which was driving the crows back into the darkness.

As the last of the birds' cries died away, Izzie collapsed sideways into James. Layah crawled forward and seized her sister's hand.

'Izzie? That was amazing!'

Izzie opened a bleary eye.

'Are you OK, Layah?' she murmured.

'I'm fine! You saved me, Iz!' Layah marvelled at her sister.

Izzie slumped against the tunnel wall, grey and dogged. Layah's heart sang with pride. Izzie the bookworm, the scone guzzler, the hero! Izzie pressed the floor with her left foot and winced.

Layah looked at James, who was panting, his dark hair wet with sweat. He seemed half in shock but he helped Layah pull Izzie upright. They balanced her between them.

'I think I may have twisted my ankle. I'm sorry.' Izzie grimaced.

'Don't be sorry,' said Layah. 'Come on. We'd better get out of here.'

The debris from the fallen ceiling had been swept further up the tunnel; they would have to clamber over it, but they should be able to make it back to the entrance.

'No! We need to save Mum!' said Izzie ardently.

'You can't carry on like this! You're a mess!' said Layah.

'So are you.' Izzie smiled at the dust in Layah's hair.

'I think we ought to go on,' interjected James. 'There might be more crows behind us – they could be waiting by the entrance – maybe there's another way out?'

Layah bit her lip, watching his eyes darting up and down the tunnel. *Don't trust him!* The warning screaming inside her.

'This way. Layah, come on,' said James, putting

an arm around Izzie's waist.

They continued down the tunnel. Layah's free hand checked the sock of arrows tied in her belt and the crossbow on her back which was, miraculously, unharmed. They staggered around a corner and came to a break where two passages led off in opposite directions; the ceiling was higher here and they could stand normally again. There was a greyish light now and Layah could see beyond the beam of her headtorch. She couldn't detect the source of the light.

'This way,' said James, pulling Izzie into the left-hand passage.

Layah staggered to keep up as James lengthened his strides, almost lifting Izzie from the floor.

'Wait! Why? How do you know it's this way?' called Layah.

'I'm trying to get us out of here!' he cried. 'There's no time t—'

Before James could finish there was a burst of artificial light. Layah squinted against the brightness as someone came marching towards them.

'Ah there you are, girls. Better late than never. Thank you, James, I'll take it from here,' said Henry Westwood, stepping forward, his teeth set in a deadly grin.

# Chapter Twenty-Five

'Layah, run!' screamed Izzie.

She shoved Layah away from Henry, back the way they had come. Anger and frustration burnt Layah's insides.

*No!* It couldn't end like this! They weren't going to be stopped by stupid Henry Westwood. She turned, one hand still tight on Izzie's wrist, but then she saw her.

Mesula was walking calmly towards them, her arms lolling lazily at her sides, her wings towering above her shoulders, her yellow eyes wide with anticipation. All the fight inside Layah shrank in a shadow of fear. She looked back to Izzie then James, who was gaping at the Vilsestra.

'You betrayed us!' yelled Layah, pushing James back against the wall before she knew what she was doing.

It was as if somehow punishing him would be enough to make the danger around them disappear. Layah's punches smarted against his arms and the corners

221

of his collarbones.

'I knew we couldn't trust you,' screamed Layah. 'You tricked us!'

Layah could sense Mesula moving in behind her and Henry bobbing uncertainly from foot to foot.

'Layah, listen!' James cried. 'Layah! I didn't—'

'Enough of this squabbling.'

Layah felt a dry, cold arm wrapping around her shoulders; she stumbled backwards, a musty scent filling her throat. Mesula's hot jaw was at her ear and Layah struggled feebly.

'I admire your spirit but even a good spirit needs to be kept in check,' whispered the Vilsestra. 'I don't think you'll be needing this.' Layah felt the crossbow pulled off her back. Mesula spun Layah to face her. The closeness of that savage face turned Layah's stomach to ice. Pallid skin pulled tight across bones, the nose and chin more like a cruel beak than human features. 'I know the story of this object,' hissed Mesula, 'the slayer of my ancestors. Oh, I know the poem. But this is nothing more than rotting wood.'

Taking the crossbow in both hands, she snapped it in two. Layah heard Izzie gasp. Their only weapon was destroyed.

'Bring the small one,' Mesula demanded of Henry.

Henry took hold of Izzie's arm. Layah was relieved to see that he was being gentle with her.

Layah tripped over her feet as Mesula dragged her into a mud-walled chamber. Thin scribbles of wire ran up the wall to a single bulb drilled into the ceiling. The walls were as tall as a two-storey building and yet the dirt and dust cocooned them like a tomb. Layah's eyes travelled over the dabs of scarlet on the floor and then up to the large stone in the centre, and there was Layah's mum.

'Mum! Mum! What's she done to you?'

Layah started shouting but she swallowed her words as she took in her mum's appearance.

Her beautiful face was grimy with dirt; her wrists and ankles were bound and a rag covered her mouth. She was straining at her bonds but her movements were feeble and exhausted.

Layah slipped to her knees, another wave of terror overpowering her. It was too late. They had failed her.

Henry, Izzie and James followed behind. Izzie was pale and floppy as Henry laid her in a corner. Fear was clouding Layah's mind and she couldn't think.

James was shaking, his eyes roaming fitfully, never resting on Mesula. She felt a twinge of hope which was soon dashed by doubt – even if James was scared it didn't mean he wasn't part of Mesula's plan.

Henry looked up at Mesula and Layah saw the sweat on his forehead.

'Tie up the small one,' barked Mesula.

'Is that really necessary?' Henry waved a hand to Izzie's bad ankle.

'Do it.'

Henry's shoulders sagged but he crouched down and tied Izzie's hands behind her back. Izzie stared helplessly ahead.

'Father! What are you doing?' James cried, striding across the chamber. 'Stop this! Why are you helping her? Just—'

James grabbed the rope from Henry's hands; his father pulled back, his face growing red.

'James! Don't be foolish,' Henry growled through bared teeth. 'Don't – get – in – volved!'

Layah noticed Mesula's pupils bulge as she watched the Westwoods. She sensed the Vilsestra tightening beside her, her wings fluttering dangerously. A warning bubbled in Layah's throat, but before she could shout, Mesula's arm rose, pointing directly at James. There was a rushing sound and James was slammed backward by a ferocious wind. He smashed against the opposite wall as his whole body was forced flat.

'This boy of yours clearly needs to be taught a lesson,' snarled Mesula, as James was battered like a twig in a storm.

'No! Stop! Stop! Please!' Henry yelped, cringing as he begged. 'Please don't hurt him. He's not a danger to your plans. I'll make sure he doesn't talk!'

Mesula flicked her arm down and the torrent of wind dispersed, puffing dust across the floor. Layah had sunk on to the ground, a ringing in her ears. Heart trembling, she looked towards James. He was moving slowly, rubbing blood and mud out of his face.

'Go to him, Westwood,' sighed Mesula lazily.

Henry dashed to his son's side and hoisted him up. James tried to shrug him off but fell back against him.

'It's the shock; he'll do as I say, I promise,' pleaded Henry. 'Here, James.' Henry unfurled another length of rope, which he pressed on his son. 'You'll see.' He glanced meekly towards Mesula. 'James, go on. It's just to keep them out of trouble.' And Henry pushed him towards Layah.

Layah watched James's feet as he lumbered over. Layah expected him to resist, to shout, but he squatted beside her, a loop of rope in his hand. He sighed then grasped her wrists. Layah squirmed away from him.

'No . . . get off me.'

'I'm sorry,' he murmured, 'I had no idea about any of this, you have to believe me. But, Layah, there's no point fighting her.'

She saw the truth in his eyes and her stomach sank. How could she have brought him and Izzie into such danger?

James pulled her wrists behind her back and wound the rope around them. But as he bent closer to tie the ends, she felt a whisper touch her cheek – 'Stay strong' – and he hid the untied ropes in her hands. He backed away and Henry threw an arm around him.

The Westwoods retreated into a corner and Layah felt the loose ropes around her wrists. James was right – there was no point fighting. Not yet.

Beneath the mind-clogging fear, a spark of defiance flickered in Layah's heart.

'Rianda's human family united,' said Mesula, surveying the three of them in turn. 'My plans are coming to a close.'

Her clawed feet flexed in the dirt. She stood in a half-crouch, the great wings quivering, every muscle tensed as if ready to pounce.

She spoke directly to Layah, tipping her head to the side.

'He is not my usual choice of accomplice but Mr Westwood's desires make him so easy to control,' she growled. 'He was willing to help trap two young girls in return for the woman he wants.'

Layah watched Henry flush pink. She felt like she was going to vomit. There was a pounding from the rock; Layah's mum was banging her heels into the stone, her eyes huge with fury. Henry stumbled to her side and seized her hand.

'Oh! Don't be angry with me, Ren!' Henry blubbered. 'This is all a misunderstanding. I didn't want anyone to get hurt!'

'You liar.' Mesula laughed softly. 'You begged me to kill her husband. You didn't care what happened to the daughters either.'

'How could you?' James was gazing in horror at his father.

Layah had been right to dislike Henry, but she hadn't expected this. Henry was still pawing at her mum's sleeve and Ren strained away from him.

'She's making it up, to keep us apart!' Henry pleaded. 'But we belong together, Ren! When we get out of this, I'll make it all up to you.'

'Oh, enough!' cawed Mesula, bored at last. 'You will never see Rianda again after tonight. Did you really think I would just hand her over to you? I know your kind; just like King Vukasin of old, you may love her now – but once you see her for who she truly is, you will despise her!'

Mesula's wings beat out behind her. The forcefield pulsed through the chamber; Layah tensed, waiting for a blow to fall. Henry didn't seem to have noticed the danger; he was still grovelling beside her mum, but James was backing into the corner beside Izzie.

Layah saw Mesula raise her hand, pointing it towards Henry. But there was a shout from behind them.

'Step away from my family, you treacherous bully!'

Layah looked up at her dad framed in the chamber entrance, splattered in mud, a shovel in his hand and thunder in his face. Hope and triumph rose in Layah's chest. He came charging into the chamber, chucking aside the shovel; he ran straight past Mesula and, with a great 'Ooof!', he punched Henry squarely on the nose.

# Chapter Twenty-Six

Layah's initial happiness faded as her dad and Henry grappled like clumsy chickens, squawking at each other. Henry's nose was bleeding as he tugged at her dad's ears and her dad batted at his hands, the two of them rolling on the dusty floor.

'You little prig, Seb! Is that the best you can do?'

'Don't touch her, you abnormal dung beetle!'

'Boffin-head!'

'Two-faced rat!'

Layah looked sideways at James, who was gazing at their dads with mild embarrassment. Mesula swooped down and – gripping them by their collars – strung up the men like shirts on a washing line; Layah's dad's glasses were dangling off one ear and the bandage on his bad leg was ripped.

'Foolish males!' snarled Mesula.

In a single swift movement she had tied them back to back, before dumping them in a corner.

'I might as well make a clean job of it,' Mesula muttered to herself. 'Boy!'

James didn't struggle as Mesula tied his wrists but he let out a groan as she kicked him on to the floor with a scaly foot. He crawled next to Izzie, whose eyes were fixed fearfully on Mesula.

'I have wasted enough energy on the males! Now . . .'

'The police are coming,' spluttered Dad. 'They've been following me. They—'

'By the time the police turn up I shall have dealt with Rianda and her daughters, and you men shall be dead in the lake,' spat Mesula, her wings bristling. She turned to face Layah. 'But we have things to discuss before then.'

'If you're so desperate to punish Mum,' stammered Layah, 'why did you even let her go in the first place?'

'Oh, but this isn't about your traitor mother,' said Mesula smoothly. 'Layah, this is about you. It has always been about you.'

Layah's mum started to go wild, writhing against her bonds, her screams muffled behind the rag. Her mum's raw fear was more terrifying than anything Layah had yet seen. All Layah could do was stare up at Mesula as she prowled across the floor to stand above her. There was nothing she could do to defend herself. She tried to speak but couldn't.

'Rianda is lost to me,' said Mesula. 'She will never live the future I planned for her. I have waited many years for this moment. I have kept watch on Rianda, as she stooped and scraped as a pitiful human. I have been most patient. I approached Westwood a few months ago, well aware of his desire for Rianda. A man's wallet can tell you so much: two photos of an old school friend and not one of his own son.' Unblinking eyes flickered to James. 'I said I could offer him Rianda, and get revenge on the man who took her from him – this spineless snail.'

Layah's dad shuffled, his ears going pink. Layah felt a fresh bout of anger strengthening her.

'I staged a dramatic reveal in Rianda's London garden,' continued Mesula, the ends of her wings slithering in the dust as she stalked back and forth. 'I frightened Rianda into thinking I was back to punish her for deserting me. But to fight me, she needed her powers: she needed to return to the Lakes. Babysitting a human is so tiresome but Westwood had his uses. Offering up his cottage, concocting his canoeing trips and island picnics – ensuring that you girls were exactly where I wanted you, so I could carry out my little games.'

Of course Henry would have known when they arrived at Westwood Manor, thought Layah. He must have security cameras all over his estate which he could access from afar. Henry was the one who had helped weave Mesula's trap.

'You were hiding the bracelet, weren't you?' snarled Layah at Henry. 'All this time, you've been hiding Mum's powers!'

'Oh no, no,' Mesula cackled, 'Westwood wasn't smart enough to think of that on his own. He had no idea of its importance. I gave him the bracelet and told him where to hide it. My Rianda would never suspect I would stoop so low as to work with a human.'

Mesula opened her claw to reveal the bracelet and placed it tantalisingly on the rock beside Layah's mum.

'Mum doesn't want to be a Vilsestra!' said Layah. 'Why can't you just let her go? She doesn't need her powers.'

'Oh, she needs them,' cawed Mesula, stretching her long neck towards Layah's mum. 'Even in her human form, she was drawn to the Lakes; she can sense them. I'm surprised it took so long for her to come back. Searching the mountains has kept her busy these last few days. Poor Mummy became quite obsessed with her hunt, leaving her little daughters alone in that draughty cottage. When Rianda finally discovered her bracelet and realised Westwood was working for me, she confronted him. The coward fled to his hotel, but I brought him back. I don't like loose ends and I needed him to call the police, to throw suspicion on your father – I'm afraid Daddy will get the blame when you three disappear.'

Layah stared up at Mesula – at the beast toying with her prey – hate and fear ricocheting inside her. All she could think of doing was to keep Mesula talking.

'Why did you let me see you,' said Layah slowly, 'that night in the garden?'

'It became clear to me that your mother had not told you of her origins,' rasped Mesula. 'I knew I must force her to tell you her story, so I led you on your own treasure hunt. I was keen to see the effect which the knowledge would have on you. Yet, Layah, I was disappointed . . . even after everything you found, you did not realise what the discovery could mean for yourselves. You cared too much about your mother's lie.'

Mesula strode to Layah's mum's side and looked down at her, reading her like an incomplete map.

'How did you know we'd follow you?' said Layah.

'I gave you enough clues to put you on track to the

island.' Mesula ruffled her feathers lazily. 'I knew you would come. You are even more stubborn than your foolish mother. I knew you would ignore the dangers, blinded by bravery.'

Layah gazed at Mesula. She'd known somewhere in the back of her mind that her whole rescue plan had been idiotic from the start. If only she'd come alone. She could have spared the others.

'What do you want from me?' Layah couldn't hold back the panic in her voice.

Mesula smiled stealthily.

'I believe you have a birthday coming up?' she growled softly. 'Thirteen years old. For a Vilsestra, thirteen is the age when her powers become fully formed. The age your mother was when she helped me murder that family.'

'She didn't murder them,' cried Layah, 'she tried to save them.'

'Those snooping Bellfords with their bird books and their butterfly nets,' spat Mesula, her features darkening. 'Your mother used great power that night. Great power she may have passed to you, Layah.' Mesula licked her lips. 'You are the daughter of a human and a Vilsestra. I admit, I have never come across it before, but Vilsestra blood is strong.'

'And what if I don't have powers?' said Layah.

'Oh, we will have to experiment,' said Mesula. 'Perhaps just one of you has been gifted. Perhaps both. I am willing to test my theory if it means expanding our clan and restoring the old Vilsestra Teachings. Perhaps you have already flexed your powers, Layah; perhaps you know what I am saying is true . . .'

'No.' Layah tried to speak calmly. 'We talked about it but we – we don't have any powers. We're just human.'

Her stomach had dropped like a stone. She should have realised it before. Layah was nothing compared to Mesula.

Mesula was shaking her head, a smile chipping across her face.

'Who defeated my crows in the tunnel?' she whispered. 'I felt the energy through the walls. I know one of you conjured a gust and it must have been strong or it would not have beaten them.'

Layah said nothing as she stared back into those terrible yellow eyes.

'Perhaps punishing the little one will loosen your tongue.' Mesula leered.

The Vilsestra drew herself up tall, her wings flicking excitedly. She turned her greedy eyes on Izzie.

Izzie was trembling in the corner, her small white face marbled with dirt.

'As Rianda knows, pain and punishment are best for drawing out the powers of a youngster. It is a shame to damage a fledgling, but I'm willing to risk it. Be still, little Izobel. The less you struggle, the less likely I am to kill you.'

Layah saw tears of fear in Izzie's eyes but then, her hands still tied behind her back, Izzie rose to stand. She stared back at the Vilsestra, swaying on her bad ankle. Ready for the pain.

Layah felt a surge of anger towards Mesula, which outshone the fear and helplessness inside her. She wasn't going to let this monster touch her sister.

As Mesula moved towards Izzie, Layah dragged her fists apart and the rope fell away. Jumping upright, Layah sprinted towards the Vilsestra – Babcia's amber pendant hot on her neck, filling her with a burning fury – her heart hitting her ribs, her feet skimming across the floor and then – she was flying. Layah felt new muscles surging from her shoulders as wings sprouted out behind her. Powerful feathered wings expanded from her in a glorious stretch. Layah hardly had time to accept what was happening before she arched into the air and her foot slammed into Mesula's jaw.

Mesula was quick to react. She was in the air, tearing at Layah's face with her fingernails, dragging Layah along in her own current. Layah was disorientated; the wall came up suddenly and slammed into her head but she pulled away and somehow found herself thrusting the fight up to the ceiling. Feathers obscured Layah's vision as she hit and blocked the flailing movement around her. A new energy was coursing through her; the heavy wings at her back were hoisting her to and fro, powerful but uncontrollable.

'Layah! Hang on!'

Upside-down Layah heard Izzie's shout of encouragement come again. James was struggling with his own ropes and Layah saw him wrench a hand free – then a wall came hurtling towards her and she ducked and twisted.

Mesula ripped the amber necklace from Layah's neck and dashed it to the floor; she caught Layah by the throat, piercing her skin. They were still locked in mid-air and Layah choked, struggling in Mesula's grasp – with her free hand she scrabbled for the arrows in her belt, but the pain was too much. There was movement below her – everyone was shouting.

'James! Here! Son!' Henry's voice bellowed above the rest and Layah saw him, still tied to her dad, shaking his jacket; a metallic object clanged on to the floor.

'Shoot them, James! Shoot both of them!'

Layah's back slammed against a wall and she heard Mesula's laughter in her ear. Layah's cheek was forced back into the dirt but she could still see James as he grabbed the gun.

'Shoot, James! Goddammit!' Henry was yelling. 'They're both monsters!'

Through her pain, Layah saw James's panic and fear shook her.

'James, help her!' Izzie screamed from out of sight.

Layah's eyes widened as James pointed the gun in her direction. For a heartbeat, their eyes met—

'Layah, keep back!' James shouted and he fired.

Layah felt Mesula's body jerk above her, the fingers loosening, as a bullet tore into her wing. Layah's sweaty hand fumbled on the stem of an arrow – but then Mesula's face loomed back over her, blood in her teeth.

'I cannot be finished by any man-made machines,' screeched the Vilsestra, the bones in her face curving into a hideous beak. 'You'll have to give in to me, Layah.'

'I don't think so,' croaked Layah, her fist tightening on the arrow. 'No one messes with my family and gets away with it!'

Memories blazed in Layah's mind – laughter and love around a kitchen table – flooding her with hope as she plunged the arrow into Mesula's heart. The Vilsestra screamed – wild and ugly – and keeled backwards out of the air. Her body hit the floor with a reverberating groan. Layah's shoulders relaxed and she floated to the ground. She felt the wings sliding away into her shoulder blades. She looked down at the body of feathers and skinny bones before her. The yellow eyes were still open but no light shone out.

Mesula was dead.

# Chapter Twenty-Seven

The sudden silence in the chamber rang in Layah's ears. Mesula's body was unnerving to look at, even now she was so still. Tentatively, the group circled around her, each stepping forward warily as if she might spring up at any moment.

Layah's dad was holding up her mum, who was shaking on weakened legs and Izzie was beside them, tears streaming down her face. James was still pointing the gun at the corpse and Henry was cowering in a corner, too afraid to move closer.

The power that had erupted inside Layah was still churning through her blood. The skin where the wings had burst from her back was tingling.

Her mum spoke first, her voice broken. 'Thank you, Layah.'

Layah's mum looked down at Mesula, no anger blurring her features, but a sad look of pity creased her eyes.

'Mum . . .'

Something seemed to tear inside Layah as she strode over to her mum and engulfed her in a hug. Layah felt Izzie's arms wrap around her waist, her dad's hand on her back, as the four of them held each other. Layah's face was buried in her mum's shoulder and, as relief cascaded over her, she blocked out everything else. For a moment everything was as it should be. They were together.

Henry's voice interrupted them. 'Well, this is hardly the time for a group hug!' he said impatiently. 'Shouldn't we be heading off before the police arrive?'

Layah's family turned to glare at him.

'You lying pig!' snarled Mum. 'You put my whole family in danger! I should have locked you up the moment I realised you were involved – I was too soft on you!'

Her mum staggered towards Henry.

'Ren! Ren!' he grovelled. 'I only did it because I love you! I was going to help you escape. That's why I took the gun – I was going to save you! I just – just hadn't gotten around to it yet. Please!'

'You're not even worth me raising my fist to hit you,' she said furiously, 'but . . .' She glanced at her family. 'I suppose we ought to take him back with us?'

'Frankly, I think it would be a fair punishment if we

left him down here!' said Dad, his arm around Izzie's shoulders.

'Oh no! I couldn't stay here! I'd just – die,' Henry yelped.

'You should say you did it,' said James.

Layah looked up at him. James was weighing the gun in his hands, a bitter expression on his face.

'The police will want an explanation,' James continued. 'If someone doesn't take the blame, they'll pin it on Mr Kosmatka. They already suspect him.'

'Is that true?' Mum said to their dad. 'Seb? The police suspect you?' She seemed mildly impressed.

'They do?' Dad stuttered. 'I mean, yes – of course! I'm a dangerous suspect!' he added, tweaking his glasses. 'I ran away from the police! They came to the cottage but I managed to escape and I tracked the girls to Westwood Manor. That's when I heard the speedboat leaving so I decided to follow it. Luckily I picked up this shovel, because I had a bit of a fight with some birds in the tunnel.'

Layah saw scratches on his neck and face.

'But how did you know where we'd gone?' asked Izzie, but Henry spoke over her.

'Kosmatka, did you break into my house?'

'I don't think you're in a position to be angry,' James

snapped at his father. 'Will you take the blame for kidnapping Ren and the girls or not?'

'And make sure you tell the police that my dad came after you and he was the one who rescued us,' added Layah, stepping beside James. 'Not a word about the Vilsestra.'

'But – but – but – think of my reputation!' protested Henry. 'What will the newspapers write?!'

There was a sudden grating sound and the whole chamber shook; clumps of dirt thudded from the ceiling and the blub flickered.

'The tunnel!' gasped Izzie.

Layah sprinted out of the chamber – there were cracks, huge as craters, in the tunnel walls and, as she watched, chunks of rock crumbled from the roof. She dashed back to the others.

'Mum! The tunnel – it's collapsing! There's no way out!' cried Layah.

'All right! I'll do it!' wailed Henry, hands cradling his head. 'I'll confess! Just don't leave me here.'

Layah ignored him and raced over to her family. 'Mum, what can we do?'

'We'll have to break out!' said Izzie, craning up at the ceiling.

'You're right. Up is our only escape,' Mum said; Layah

could see her fighting against pain and fatigue. 'James, pass me the bracelet.'

With the bracelet on her wrist, Layah's mum's eyes blazed yellow and she breathed deeply. Despite her injuries, she pulled herself up and her wings erupted from her shoulders; her arms rose and the dust in the chamber swirled upwards.

'Layah,' she called, 'do you remember that summer at Babcia's when we did the book balancing in the garden?'

'This is hardly the time to reminisce about the good old days!' screamed back Layah, the wind howling louder and louder.

'I need you to remember what it was like balancing those books on your head!' Mum yelled. 'You need to keep your shoulders balanced to control your wings. Imagine the books – it'll help you fly straight. You can do it!'

'I can help too, Mum,' said Izzie, stretching out her hands and causing a breeze to rumble across the floor.

'You too?' Their mum grinned, eyes gleaming with pride. 'We'll do it together! Seb – take the rope – tie it around my waist and you, Henry and James, need to hold on! I'll carry your weight. Layah, you hold on

244

tight to Izzie – and Iz, I need you to push upwards.'

The dust and wind spiralled faster and faster, making Layah feel dizzy. She clutched her mum's hand. There was a crash and Layah turned to see the entrance to the chamber crushed under an avalanche; boulders the size of bowling balls were thundering from the ceiling.

'Layah, focus! I need you to rise on my count,' shouted Mum. 'I know you can do it. Hold on, everyone! Three, two, one!'

It was too quick for her to think – Layah felt the wings burst from her again and her feet take off from the ground. The ceiling cracked under the force of Mum and Izzie's whirlwind and they shot upwards, Layah's arm almost jerking out of its socket as her mum dragged her onwards. The wind ahead of them smashed through the dirt and earth. The wings at her back beating wildly, Layah tried to balance – picturing the sunny garden in Poland, wobbling down the lawn, feeling the weight of the books – she felt the wings straighten up, beating powerfully. Layah's arms were around Izzie's waist and Izzie was pointing upwards, vibrating with power as she helped clear the earth above them with a tornado of wind.

Layah peeked down and saw her dad, Henry and James clinging to the rope attached to her mum; beyond them there was blackness. And then the earth above them burst open and they were tumbling out into the cool, wet air and Layah felt her wings retract to nothing.

'Layah, get up!' she heard Dad shouting.

He grabbed her hand, just as the ground began to shake. Together they leapt on to solid land and Layah looked back.

The hole which they had just created was imploding in on itself. There was a shuddering grunt as the earth poured back into the opening and tumbled into the cave below. Soon the hole was hidden under the fall of dirt and rolling rocks.

Layah looked around at the others. They were dotted about the hillside, dirty and panting, but all unharmed. They were free!

The six of them – bruised, battered and limping – made their way through the trees in the direction of the jetty. Layah was supporting her mum; their ascent from the chamber had drained her so much, she could barely speak. As they crested the hill, Layah became aware of the new noises surrounding them. Avery Island was crackling with radio voices and blue-white searchlights combing the shrubbery. The police had arrived.

As they emerged from the treeline, Layah could see the jetty below. The dawn had broken, washing the scene in pale light. Three boats bobbed in the water: the Vellamo speedboat, the police patrol boat and the battered old Wayfarer, *Jiya*, from the Westwoods' lawn.

'Kosmatka! Did you sail here in that rotten water bath?' Henry grumbled.

The jetty below suddenly erupted with shouts and spluttering megaphones, as the people turned to stare as the six of them descended the slope. The patrol boat was dazzling them with a spotlight.

'It's the London family and Henry Westwood!'

'Henry Westwood! Well, I'll be!'

As they reached the crowd, Henry stepped forward, arms raised above his head.

'Do not be alarmed!' he called. 'I am no longer dangerous! In a moment of madness, I stole away my old school friend – blinded by my love – and her two daughters! Until I was thwarted by . . . um . . . this man.' Henry nudged his head in the vague direction of their dad – all eyes, and a couple of cameras, turned towards Seb Kosmatka. 'But now,' Henry continued, 'I know how foolish—'

'I'm from the *Newbeck Inquirer*!' called a pimply woman, advancing with a pen and notepad.

'No interviews, please,' sighed Henry, with a modest wave of his hand.

'Not you, sir, I was talking to Mr Kosmatka,' interjected the reporter, 'Mr Kosmatka, how does it feel to be the hero of the hour? To have rescued your wife and daughters?'

Henry's face sank into a sour pout.

'Well . . .' Layah's dad gazed nervously at the keen faces before him. 'Um . . . no complaints.'

The reporters started scribbling at once.

'Err . . .' Their dad fumbled for words. 'But I couldn't have done it without my magnificent daughters, who – um – left the clues to this – um – slimy man's destruction!'

Izzie rolled her eyes at Layah as their dad blinked and babbled, turning his apologetic smile to the flashing cameras. Layah laughed. It felt like a balloon was swelling inside her chest as she realised that she had not smiled in a very long time.

# CHAPTER TWENTY-EIGHT

Next morning, the *Newbeck Inquirer* ran with the following headline:

## 'NO COMPLAINTS':
### *HERO DAD SAVES THE DAY*

The newspaper had been placed in the centre of the breakfast table at Rook Cottage. It was surrounded by celebratory breakfast items: bacon, tomatoes, garlic mushrooms, baked beans, stacks of toast, jam jars, Nutella, hot chocolate, a large pot of tea, an even larger cafetière, their mum's lumpy pancakes, freshly made blueberry *pierogi* and a bowl of leftover cheesy nibbles.

Technically it was closer to lunch than breakfast.

The police officers who had searched Westwood Manor, DCI Swift and her deputy DC Blackmore, had eventually separated Layah's dad from the journalists. Their dad had treated the press to a full-colour description of his rescue, which apparently involved him swinging down on a grapevine and defeating Henry with a toothbrush and a plastic fork.

Rook Cottage was still in a shambolic state. Binbags of rubble cluttered the upstairs corridor and the bedsheet still covered the hole in their mum's bedroom. The four of them had slept in Layah and Izzie's room, their parents squished on the floor in between the beds. Even though her dad snored, it had been the best night's sleep Layah had ever had. Despite her many bruises and cuts, her whole body felt lighter as she looked around the breakfast table at her family.

'Pass the jam, Layah, please?' Izzie nudged her.

'Bilberry? Raspberry? Or mystery orange one?' said Layah.

'All, please,' replied Izzie, who was making a kind of pancake wrap with everything on the table.

Their mum was reading out the newspaper article and Layah turned back to listen.

'Oh, now this is a good bit!' said Mum. '"*I vow Mr Westwood will pay for what he's done to my family!*" *promised Mr Kosmatka, as he carried his unconscious youngest daughter to safety* – did you really make a *vow*?' She laughed.

'I don't know,' said Dad, spilling his coffee as he

reached for more bacon. 'It's all a bit of a blur, really – who knows what I was saying.'

'And I wasn't unconscious,' added Izzie. 'Such sloppy reporting these days!'

They all laughed.

'Jokes aside, I want to know the real rescuers' story,' said Mum. 'Izzie, Layah, I am absolutely mad at both of you. I can't believe you put yourselves in so much danger but I can't deny I'm very impressed. How did you do it?'

'I suppose it all starts with Lowesdale School,' said Layah, Izzie beaming beside her.

The sisters embarked upon their retelling with gusto, explaining all about the photograph, Layah's trip to Newbeck, their late-night escapade to Westwood Manor, visiting Teddington Speckleback's emporium and the mission to Avery Island. Layah watched Izzie waving around a forkful of mushrooms as she described them running away from the crows in the tunnel and felt warm with pride. She couldn't have done it without her.

'I can't believe you went on James's scooter without asking me first!' tutted Mum, only half-annoyed. 'Vespas can be really dangerous!'

'More dangerous than blasting out of a hillside?' Layah grinned roguishly.

'I had a scooter when I was teenager,' said Dad dreamily. 'I took your mum for a spin once or twice!'

'That was an old bicycle with mouldy handlebars.' Their mum laughed. 'And it still had stabilisers!'

Layah watched them laughing – her dad's glasses clouding up, making her mum laugh even harder – but with a jolt she remembered why their dad hadn't come to the Lakes in the first place. Panic flooded her.

'Are you still getting divorced?' she blurted out.

Izzie dropped her pancake and the smiles faded from their parents' faces. They looked at each other.

'No. That was never on the cards,' said Mum carefully. 'We're going to try and work stuff out.'

'Work stuff out?' repeated Layah.

'Things will need to change,' said Mum. 'No more secrets. I need to learn to be more open with your dad – with all of you. And your dad's going to stop working on the weekends.'

Layah's eyes turned to her dad. He was examining his plate of *pierogi*. 'After Babcia died, I think I went into hibernation,' he said quietly. 'I thought work was the answer – keeping myself busy so I didn't need to think about anything. I was wrong.' At last he looked up at his daughters. 'The truth is, my life is a puzzle without you girls; it just doesn't make sense. And I'm sorry.'

Layah gave a jerky nod and looked down into her hot chocolate. The fog of frustration she'd been feeling towards her dad was clearing; she supposed she ought to give him a second chance. She wouldn't mind having her old dad back.

Her mum patted her dad's hand and he blinked rather fast behind his glasses.

'When someone is prepared to fight for you,' Mum said, 'to follow you into danger and brave all the odds to keep you safe, you know you've got something worth fighting for.'

James Westwood floated into Layah's mind and she was engulfed by guilt. It was her fault that his life had been turned upside down. She wished she'd had a moment to speak to him, but it had been impossible with the police swarming all over them. She'd never got a chance to say thank you. It wasn't his fault he had a nasty megalomaniac father. He was probably wishing he'd never met her. He probably thought she was a freak – a monster! – just like his father had said.

'Layah, are you OK?' said Izzie.

They were all looking at her.

'It's just, well . . . James!' muttered Layah. 'What's going to happen to him?'

'Well, as long as bloomin' Henry Westwood get what he deserves, I'm a happy camper,' said Dad, raising his coffee mug in a mock 'toast'.

Layah rolled her eyes at him. 'But it's not fair on James,' she said. 'If Henry goes to prison, his whole life is ruined! All he did was help us.'

'Henry was willing to put us all in harm's way,' said Mum, 'but I'll see what we can do. Of course you're worried about your friend.'

'Yeah – no – well, we're not friends.' Layah's voice wobbled. 'I . . . I pushed him away . . . like I always do. He probably thinks I'm a freak anyway.'

'We're not freaks!' protested Izzie, three colours of jam on her cheeks.

'Layah, don't be so hard on yourself,' Mum said, and Layah shrugged. 'Mesula said Vilsestra power needs pain and punishment to reveal it, but she was wrong. Love and loyalty – those are the powers which helped you save each other.'

Layah's eyes were itching.

'There was one thing Mesula was right about, though,' said Mum. 'I have always yearned for my powers, for the bracelet, all these years. So, I've decided something.'

Her mum took the bracelet from her pocket and stood

up. She walked to the broken kitchen door, which they'd patched up using the bathroom rug, and opened it to let the morning air in. Then, with sudden strength, their mum smashed the bracelet against the door frame. It splintered into fragments and there was a rushing noise, a stirring of leaves in the garden and a distant crackle; then there was silence. Their mum took a long, deep sigh.

'You took back your powers?' said Izzie. 'Why? Will you use them again?'

'I may never use them.' Her mum smiled. 'But I am a Vilsestra and I cannot ignore it. Being yourself is the best you can hope to be.'

Their mum kissed Izzie's head and squeezed Layah's hand. Layah felt something warm in her palm; looking down, she found Babcia's amber pendant, glowing like a golden sun, attached to a new silver chain.

'You saved it from the chamber?' said Layah.

Her mum nodded.

'Mr Speckleback said the amber had protective powers,' said Layah; she was struck by an idea. 'Did Babcia know? Did she know what you were?'

'Your dad's mum was a wise woman.' Their mum smiled. 'She must have suspected that there was evil in my past. Amber is a human superstition. I may have strengthened them up with my own Vilsestra protection.'

Her mum took Layah's pendant and pressed a fingernail into the side; the pendant clicked open.

'A lock of Vilsestra hair,' said Mum, showing them the dark brunette coil inside. 'My hair, for luck and courage.'

Layah fastened the necklace around her neck and felt the heat from the pendant against her heart.

'Wait a moment, we still don't know how Dad knew to go to Westwood Manor,' said Izzie, 'and how he escaped the police?'

Their dad grinned sheepishly.

'Funny you should ask,' Dad said. 'Truth be told, I had a bit of help. I would have snoozed through the whole night if it hadn't been for the note.'

He rummaged in his pockets and Layah and Izzie leant forward.

'It was thrown through the living room window,' he said, holding up a scrunched piece of paper. 'Woke me up five minutes before the police were banging on the door! Gave me just enough time to sneak out the back – I used your mum's pyjamas as a camouflage and crept across the back lawn to avoid them. But they did hear me running away up the road and chased me to the Manor. I probably shouldn't have been humming my own theme tune . . .'

Trying not to be distracted by the image of her dad

wearing their mum's pyjamas, Layah bent to examine the note. Written in lopsided writing:

Watch out for police.
Girls in Westwood Manor. Go!

'I knew it was telling the truth because it was wrapped in this.'

Their dad held up a torn buckle, which Layah didn't recognise, but Izzie let out a knowing sigh.

'I think I can explain this mystery,' said Mum, her smile widening. 'Get your shoes on, girls! There's one more secret I need to share with you.'

The sun was brighter than Layah had seen it during their whole stay. Their mum was driving the car they'd hired to go back to London. The car rocketed along like a moving greenhouse, smelling of hot leather and their mum's flowery perfume. A blue sky shone overhead and skylarks soared high above them.

'Right! Here we are.'

Layah unglued her forehead from the window. They had pulled up right outside Lowesdale School.

'I've been doing some detective work of my own,' said Mum. 'Come on!'

Layah and Izzie trailed behind as their mum strode through the iron gates, which were propped open, into the sun-filled courtyard beyond.

'Mum's enjoying this.' Izzie grinned, limping on her bandaged ankle.

The paramedic had said it was only twisted and the bruise would go down in a few days, but Layah could see Izzie was in more pain than she let on.

*Tap-tap. Tap-tap.* Layah stopped short. Mor Hemlock was rocking towards them. Layah glanced at their mum, who greeted the caretaker with a smile.

'Moreen has been incredibly kind.' Their mum beckoned the girls forward. 'She's been helping me research Lauren . . .' She glanced quickly at Mor Hemlock. '. . . my *cousin* Lauren's life here,' she lied smoothly. 'Moreen, these are my daughters I told you about: Layah and Izzie.'

The caretaker gave both sisters a hard stare.

'Shall we?' said Mum and Mor Hemlock jerked her head and stamped away.

They followed her and Layah's eye was caught by the sinister wind chimes in the trees that she had noticed during their break-in. They weren't sinister at all; in fact, they were birdfeeders and two sparrows were flapping around them.

Mor Hemlock paused in a far corner of the school yard where the light gleamed brightest. There was a stone plaque attached to the wall, a black marble square with gold words etched upon it. Mor Hemlock wiped a cloth over the monument, then stepped back.

Layah knew what it would say before she read it.

> IN LOVING MEMORY OF
>
> # LAUREN MARY BELLFORD
> STUDENT AND FRIEND
>
> AND HER PROUD PARENTS
> ## FRANK AND JANET BELLFORD

'I think of them every day,' whispered Mum. 'I wanted us to come here to remember them. I hate that I benefited from their deaths, but without Lauren's name I would never have escaped. Our family would never have existed.'

The three of them stood for a few minutes, a little breeze catching at their hair and the hem of their mum's dress. Layah thought about the girl in that grainy school photograph. The girl Layah had felt such a strong connection to, who had turned out to be the key to their mum's hidden past. Lauren's tragic death had meant a new life for a scared girl, trapped in the service of a monster.

There was a zip-squeak and Layah jumped to see Izzie rummaging in her rucksack. Izzie extracted the photograph of L. Bellford and her tennis team and held it out to Mor Hemlock, who took it with hooked fingers.

'You threw the notes at James and at our dad, didn't you?' said Izzie.

Mor Hemlock gave a crooked smile, the light dancing in her white eyes. Layah noticed the bronze buttons on her coat, the same as the button which James had found in his note.

'You weren't trying to stop us last night, outside Mr Speckleback's,' said Layah. 'You were trying to help us?'

Mor Hemlock bowed her head.

'You are friends of the birds,' she said, her voice soft as a fluttering moth. 'I help the wild as I would a friend.'

'Just like you helped the Lowesdale Stranger all those years ago,' said Izzie, and their mum flashed her a warning look. 'You put the food parcels in the forest. You wanted to care for them, like you care for the birds.'

Layah felt ashamed for judging the strange woman whose kindness had given her mum hope. She'd been a good friend all this time. From the way she looked at Ren, Layah was sure that Mor Hemlock knew exactly who their mum was.

There was a rumble and a blur of red zoomed past the school gates. James!

'I've got to go!' exclaimed Layah, and she pelted out of the iron gates; the red Vespa was wheezing up towards the high street.

There was one task yet to complete and it was now or never.

Layah raced up the hill, past the Old Singer Tea Room, dodging the yapping dog from the post office, swerving through a group of ramblers . . . but the Vespa had disappeared. Hot and panting, she stumbled to a stop.

She looked up as the bookshop door opened. James stepped out into the sun.

'James! I . . . wait!'

Layah puffed up to him, her heart hammering and her legs like jelly.

'Layah – what's wrong? Has something happened? Is Mesula alive?' James grabbed her shoulders. 'Layah! What has she done to you?'

'Nothing to do with Mesula,' panted Layah, 'I'm just – out of breath!'

James let out sigh of relief. There was a dark scab across his cheek, a souvenir from their adventure.

Layah took a great breath and said, 'James, I just want to say – thank you for everything you did for me and Izzie and I'm sorry I ever suspected you of working against us! And sorry for punching you in the tunnel . . . You've been the best! And I – I wanted to ask if you'd consider . . . maybe . . . being friends? When someone is willing to risk everything and go on an adventure with you, you want that person on your team. I know I kept pushing you away, but I'm here now, if you need someone to talk to, someone to trust. OK – um – that's all.'

Layah squinted up at him, waiting for the mocking comments to fall, but James's face opened in a smile.

'I didn't exactly make it easy for you to trust me.' He shrugged. 'Sorry if I was a bit of a snooty idiot.'

'Only a little bit.' Layah smirked. 'So what are you going to do now?'

'You know your parents aren't pressing charges against my father?' he said. 'I just heard. So Father probably won't go to prison but his reputation is going to be in the dirt! I'm back to school in a few weeks but I'm going to stay with my uncle Jonny in Rome first – he's a good one – and my mum's coming to visit so I'll get to see her – she's furious with Father . . .' He paused. 'And I wanted to apologise too for hesitating in the chamber,' he said, eyes cast down. 'I was just panicked. I would never have – I mean – I don't think you're a monster! I think . . . well, actually, I think you're kind of the coolest person I've ever met.'

'So you don't think I'm a freak?' said Layah warily.

'No.' His eyes sparkled. 'In fact, I wanted to give this to you. It's an early birthday present.' He held up a book.

'*An Encyclopaedia of Birds in Europe*.' Layah glanced up at him. 'Is this supposed to be a joke?'

'It was an attempt at a joke. Figured you ought to start getting to know your bird relatives.' He grinned, and she snorted a laugh.

She folded back the pages and saw, on the final page, a handwritten entry had been added.

Half-Vilsestra-half-human: Female. Determined, wilful and strong. Stabs you with an arrow if you stand in her way. Fiercest friend I've ever had. P.S. Hates wetsuits.

Layah looked up at him, feeling brighter than she had all day.

'And for the record,' said James, 'I actually think it's rather exciting that the Lowesdale Stranger turned out to be real!'

'I thought you didn't believe in village gossip,' teased Layah.

'I guess I've got to start believing in something.' He laughed. 'Now I've got a friend like you.'

Layah beamed. She rushed forward and hugged him. It must have been the first time in his life that James Westwood had been left speechless.

Layah strode down to Lowesdale Lake, basking in the sunlight. The heat beat down on the woolly-socked walkers and the chattering families. Layah found that she'd grown fond of Lowesdale, the wild beauty and mystery of the mountains. She smiled, thinking of Mor Hemlock and her kindness to the creatures of the Lakes.

As she reached the lake, she saw Izzie coming towards her, her own amber necklace glinting cheerfully as she waved two ice creams in Layah's direction.

'Mum's gone to give Mr Speckleback the bits of crossbow back,' said Izzie, passing over one of the cones. 'Vanilla and coconut – from that place on the corner.

Shame we won't get a chance to try all the flavours.'

Layah and Izzie set off in the direction of the Boating Centre, eating their ice creams and watching the boats in the sunlight. Izzie was still limping along, but she had a pink flush in her cheeks and her eyes were bright again.

'It's been an odd holiday, hasn't it?' Layah yawned.

'The food's been good,' said Izzie, licking her ice cream thoughtfully. Then she asked, 'Do you think there are any more of them? Any more Vilsestra?'

'Mesula didn't seem to think so,' said Layah, 'or she wouldn't have tried so hard to recruit us. She thought she was saving the species.'

'It's rather sad really,' continued Izzie. 'The end of something, I mean.'

'What do you think Babcia would have thought about all of this?' said Layah.

'I think she would have loved it!' Izzie grinned. 'I mean, she loved a good mystery, didn't she?'

Layah thought of Babcia – her life spent hunting for lost poems and ancient legends – yes, she'd have loved having two Vilsestra granddaughters.

'Do you think we'll get a chance to use our powers?' asked Izzie, nibbling her cone.

Layah shrugged her shoulders; it seemed impossible

265

to think that wings had sprouted out of them.

'Mum says we can carry on as normal,' said Layah. 'She said our powers just sort of sit inside us. Frankly, I'm not that fussed. It's just nice to know they're there, you know?'

They stopped walking and looked out across the water. Two boys were racing each other in kayaks. The older was charging ahead, splashing madly with his paddle, his smaller friend calling after him.

'Yeah, I guess,' said Izzie, watching the boys pensively. 'I don't think I'm too bothered about using my powers either. I hardly think they're going to be useful at school! Although they could come in handy in the future.'

Layah watched Izzie breathe softly and a flurry of ripples darted out across Lowesdale Lake, picking up the small boy's kayak in its wake and pushing him forward, so that he outstripped his friend with a gleeful yelp. Izzie looked round at Layah and grinned guiltily.

'Y'know what?' said Layah. 'I think you're going to do just fine in secondary school.'

'You ever doubted me?' asked Izzie, bemused.

Layah laughed and linked her arm with her sister's.

'Come on, Iz.' Layah grinned. 'Let's get one more slice of cake. I'm certainly in the mood for the peanut-butter fudge.'

The two sisters walked back towards the Boat Café, the lake glinting beside them. Above them a pair of crows dived and soared, surfing the rich blue sky.

# EPILOGUE

Musty light played across the cluttered room as Layah's mum pushed back the curtain to Teddington Speckleback's emporium. The brief shiver of light illuminated the dark eyes of the stuffed birds and the emerald-blue gleam of a peacock's feather.

In the sudden gloom, she could just about pick out the clunky forms of furniture and shadowed wisps of feathers. No human presence made itself known but the room seemed busy with eyes, watching and waiting.

She stepped forward and placed the case containing a few shards of the broken crossbow and the two remaining feathered arrows on a clear tabletop.

She laid a hand thoughtfully upon the case. Considering for a moment.

'Teacher, are you? Come calling after your girls?'

Ren spun around and observed Mr Speckleback perched in a corner, a scrapbook of feathers open on his lap.

'They were good girls, no problems here!'

'I've come to return the . . . the items which you kindly gave to my daughters,' said Ren briskly. 'They wanted me to say thank you and let you know how useful it was for their . . . school project.'

Mr Speckleback remained in his corner, watching her with widening eyes.

She brushed back a strand of hair and continued coolly. 'I'm sorry to say that one item is a little damaged but I can pay for any inconvenience caused. Just let me know how much and I'll—'

'No payment. No payment.' Mr Speckleback gazed more intently. 'No price. For meeting you will be enough. It's been so long since we had such a beautiful stranger in Lowesdale.'

'Well, if you're sure,' said Ren curtly. 'Thank you.'

'And did they succeed?' Mr Speckleback was gazing at her. 'The sisters? The school projects? Both assignments finished?'

She looked at him for a second, disgust tightening the corners of her mouth.

'Yes. Both gone.' She took a step towards the exit.

'The Bellfords were explorers; they were not meddlers,' Mr Speckleback murmured in a feathered whisper. 'They meant no harm.'

He was watching her curiously, his head tipped to one side.

'I – I don't know what you mean – but thank you again.' Ren turned and shoved her way towards the dark curtain.

Mr Speckleback's chair creaked as he adjusted his position, curling his body to watch her. Layah's mum gave him a brief smile before rolling the curtain aside and escaping into the sunshine.

'Goodbye, my dear.' Mr Speckleback's eyes were fixed on the unfurling curtain. 'And good luck.'

A sudden breeze circled the room, jangling the ropes of hanging feathers, rifling through the papers on the desks and fluffing the wings of two stuffed crows; sunlight flickered across their beaded eyes as the curtain fell back into place and the room was left in darkness.

# GLOSSARY

**Avery Island:** From the zoologoical word aviary which mean a cage for birds (aves). So the island is literally called Bird Island!

**Babcia:** Pronounced *bap-t-cha*. Polish for Grandmother.

**Barszcz soup:** Pronounced *bar-sh-ch*. A bright purple Polish soup made from beetroot. Often eaten on Polish Christmas Eve with *pierogi* floating in the soup!

**Hazelnut Tort:** Pronounced *t-or-t*. A flourless Polish cake made from ground hazelnuts and almonds. Often covered in chocolate or coffee icing.

**Krakow:** Pronounced *krack-k-ov*. One of the oldest cities in Poland which dates back to the 7th Century.

**Pierogi:** Pronounced *pie-ro-gee*. A classic Polish dumpling made from dough – somewhere between Asian dumplings and ravioli pasta. It is often filled with mushrooms, sauerkraut (cabbage) or cheesy potato before being boiled in water and (if you want a real treat) fried in butter. You can also have sweet *pierogi* filled with blueberries.

There is a Pierogi Festival in Krakow every spring.

**Ren:** A wren is a tiny brown bird. For such a small bird it has a remarkably loud voice – rather like Layah and Izzie's mum.

**Rianda:** Pronounced *Ree-and-a*. This name is taken from Welsh medieval mythology; Rhiannon is a goddess of birds and horses.

**Vellamo** (the Westwoods' speedboat): The name taken from a Finnish Goddess of the sea, lakes and storms.

**Vilsestra:** Pronounced *Vil-sess-t-ra*. In Ancient Slavic (or Ancient Polish) poetry, there is a creature called the *Vila* or *Vile*: a woman-like spirit closely associated with birds and nature. Some historians believe that the name is in fact a shortened version of the creature's full name – but this name has been lost to history. I have created a new name for these creatures. In Ancient Slavic, *vil-* means supernatural and *-sestra* means sister, to create 'supernatural sister'. Who knows, perhaps Vilsestra is the real name those historians were searching for . . . Many other woman-bird creatures exist in European Mythology and Folklore, including the Old Norse Valkyire.

# Acknowledgements

I have always wanted to be an author. For as long as I can remember there have been stories in my head.

One day I sat down (probably in my pyjamas) and wrote the first line of the story which would become *The Bird Singers*. I had no idea where this story would take me. I had no idea that Layah and Izzie's adventure would one day turn into a published book.

So many people have helped to make my dream come true. I have so many thank-you's to give.

Thank you to my agent, Louise Lamont, for reading a draughty manuscript on a stormy election night and seeing the potential hidden amongst my messy, overly descriptive text. You are the most incredible, thoughtful, supportive agent in the world. You helped me find my voice as an author.

Thank you to Anne McNeil, Publishing Director, who decided to take a chance on me. Thank you for understanding the heart of this story and showing me that Layah needed to accept that Izzie is growing up. Little sisters can be heroes too.

Thank you to my editor, Jenna Mackintosh, for your creative insights and good humour. You are the greatest steady-handed captain of *The Bird Singers* ship and have made this whole experience incredible.

Thank you to dynamite designer, Michelle Brackenborough, for turning my story into the most beautiful book. Thank you to Paola Escobar for creating the most exquisite cover – a true work of art – and thank you to Kristyna Litten for mapping out the Lowesdale of my mind.

Thank you to Becca Allen, Ruth Girmatsion and Adele Brimacombe for your eagle-eyed proofreading and insightful comments. You have made my book better at every stage.

Thank you to publicity queen Emily Thomas, and marketing whiz Felicity 'Flic' Highet; to Nic Goode for selling this book, to Tracy Philips for handling the rights; to Hilary Murray Hill for welcoming me into the Hachette Children's Group family. Thank you to everyone at HCG who has played a part in *The Bird Singers* journey!

Special thanks to Mattie Whitehead for being the first person to say 'you are a writer'; David Sanger who told me to keep going; John McLay for planting the seeds; Lucy Pearse for your generous wisdom.

Thank you to inspirational author friends for selflessly offering their support and advice: Abi Elphinstone, Katie Tsang, Liz Kessler, Michelle Harrison, Emma Carroll,

A.F. Steadman, Ayisha Malik, Steven Butler and everyone in the author community who has supported me.

Thank you to all my friends who have encouraged and believed in me – to old friends, school friends, uni friends, publishing friends, family friends and passing cheerleaders.

Thank you to my family – Mum, Dad and my younger sister, Alice – without your care and encouragement this story about family, bravery and love would never have existed.

Finally thank you to you, the reader of this book. If you too have stories in your head and long to be an author, keep writing and know that one day your dreams will come true.

AUTHOR PHOTOGRAPH © YELLOWBELLY

# EVE WERSOCKI MORRIS

Eve grew up in North London and has been making up stories
her whole life. Despite being diagnosed with dyslexia aged 12, she
has not let that stop her literary ambitions and wrote her first full
novel aged 13. She volunteers with Coram Beanstalk Literacy Charity
as a reading helper for children, and has written book reviews for
*Stylist*, *The Times Literary Supplement* and the *Bookseller*.

Eve's grandparents came to the UK in 1946 as Polish refugees
and were placed in Staffordshire. Her grandmother was born in
Sanok in the mountains of Poland. Eve celebrates her Polish
heritage on Christmas Eve with *barszcz* soup, *pierogi*, pickled
*śledzie* and hazelnut *tort*. Her fascination with European
myths and fairy tales have inspired her debut children's
book, *The Bird Singers*.

@MzEvieMo @eve_wersocki